VIA Folios 75

THE POPE STORIES AND OTHER TALES OF TROUBLED TIMES

THE POPE STORIES

AND

OTHER TALES OF TROUBLED TIMES

GEORGE GUIDA

BORDIGHERA PRESS

Library of Congress Control Number: 2012936114

Printed in the United States.

Published by
BORDIGHERA PRESS
John D. Calandra Italian American Institute
25 W. 43rd Street, 17th Floor
New York, NY 10036

VIA Folios 75
ISBN 978–1–59954–037–5

ACKNOWLEDGEMENTS

Thanks to the editors of the following journals, in which earlier versions of these stories appear:

American Fiction, "The New Pope"
J Journal, "Rome"
Voices in Italian Americana, "Angel Boy" and "Killing the Pope"

Thanks also to the editors of *J Journal,* for nominating "Rome" for a Pushcart Prize; and to the judges of the New York City College of Technology Writing Awards for Faculty and Administration, who awarded their 2009 First Prize to "The Imbecile Professor (A Student's Defense)" and their 2010 Third Prize to "In Flight."

And special thanks to my wife, Denise Scannell-Guida, for believing in me and encouraging me to keep this work alive; to Gerry LaFemina and Lee Kostrinsky, for their fellowship; to Chris Cesare, for his art and especially his friendship; to Joanna Clapps Herman and Bill Herman, for their affection, laughter and support; to my students, for keeping me honest; to my publisher, Bordighera Press, for the care; and to my parents, Mary and George Guida, my sisters, Valerie Rose and Deborah Ferguson, my niece, Olivia Lee Ferguson, and my son, Bradley Guida, for their inspiration and love.

FOR DENISE AND BRADLEY

THE POPE STORIES

AND

OTHER TALES OF TROUBLED TIMES

TABLE OF CONTENTS

KILLING THE POPE

How would my mother react if I accidentally killed the Pope?

She'd sit at the dining room table and wait for my father to come in. He'd be out in his garage workshop, walnut-staining a baroque shelf for the porcelain statuettes of Italian *contadini* my mother's wealthy brother let her have when his tastes changed and he started collecting clay figurines of Mexican *campesinos*. She does not know who made them or what you call these peasant curios she has had for twenty years now, but she knows they deserve a grand shelf of their own.

She would sit and wait for my father to come in from completing the masterpiece. Her gaze fixed on the opaque side door window, she would absentmindedly stir a cup of coffee the way she stereotypically stirs a four-gallon pot of tomato sauce: apron binding her middle-aged girth, wrist locked, she swirling the giant wooden spoon from the shoulder, as if conjuring a pagan god from an ancient cauldron. Finally, my father would appear, groaning and stretching his trick knee, rubbing it through the old slacks he always wears in the shop. She would bite her lower lip. He would pull the door closed behind him, pull the boots from his aching feet, revealing dress socks pulled halfway up his calves. Silently, he would limp to the head of the dining room table, sit blank-faced, and wait for a cup of coffee. My mother would stare at him with his eyes averted to the bay window and front lawn beyond, fixed on the white plaster-of-Paris donkey and cart near the cypress shrubs, until she could no longer bear the silence.

"Guess what your son did, Pattelli?"

"That's right, Dad," I'd tell him later on the phone, "next thing I knew, there was the Pope lying on the ground. Blood? No, not too much. I'd've thought, you know, a lot more, him being a religious icon and all. But what did Mom say about it? No, of course not! It was an accident."

My sister Delores would understand.

"Sure, I believe you. I saw of one of my shows — *Rachel*, I think — I saw where some lady said she was possessed by the soul of the guy who killed some religious guy in England a long time ago. Are you possessed?"

Let's say I were able to get away from this American city and take a walk through the Vatican piazza. I'm walking along when someone yells, "*BOMBA!*" Until that moment caught up in the Pope's saying Mass from a balcony of one of his apartments, the assembled faithful panic, turning in flight from the Holy See's *palazzo* and basilica. Out of the corner of my eye, I see a suspicious black cylinder on the ground near the stolen Egyptian obelisk. On pure instinct, I pick it up, run in the direction of Bernini's colonnade, and hurl the *bomba* as far as I can. Unfortunately, I hurl it at the *palazzo* housing the papal apartments. The Pope is blown from his perch.

"Your brother killed the Pope," my mother, like a little girl in a confessional, who admits to the priest everyone's sins but her own, would inform Delores. This, as my sister would be sitting around the table, working on seconds of Mom's attempt at cultural pluralism: a mélange of *past' e fagiol'* and chicken teriyaki.

"Um. . . ," Delores would begin, as she choked down cannellini beans and water cress. "I heard. You believe it? My brother!"

My mother would bite her lower lip again, and stare at the black plastic rosary beads she's had all her life but hasn't used since high school. She would call her more traditionally devout sister-in-law for advice: "Girlie, what kind of a novena would you make for this?" Later, she would ask my father to string her a new rosary: six feet long, each bead a massy charm of ivory. She'd say a prayer for this and every other sin I'd ever committed, including "ruining my Christmas party with that *spusty putann'*, you self-centered little *strunz'*."

It's not at all clear how killing the Pope would sit with my father. I mean that I'm not certain of his papal loyalties. He does keep in his workshop, taped to the metallic tool cabinet above his vice and chisels, a blanched eight-by-ten of Il Papa on his last American tour, so he might think it was wrong, what I did. But he wouldn't get emotional about it. He wouldn't scold me. When the son of an Italian father reaches a certain age — fourteen, for argument's sake — the father, if he's a good father, leaves aside scolding and punishment for the more effective tactics of disappointed suggestion and reminiscence.

"Ah, Son, did you have to kill him? Not that I wanna say you had to like him, because, to tell you the truth, the first few years aside, this particular Pope hasn't impressed me too much either. But years ago, we just kept it to ourselves. If we didn't like the Pope, we went fishing on Sundays or played cards, *brisc'*. We let the women pray. And I'll tell you, Son, my friends and I never woulda laid a hand on Pius the Twelfth."

If I were to kill the Pope, my friends in Italy would need to hear about it. "*Veramente?*" they'd marvel. "*Tu?* We always thought it would be an Italian. *Ma, Bravo!* Good for you. Look at this *bastardo American'*. *A managgia!*"

Assuming the Italian authorities wouldn't hold the whole imbroglio against me, I'd like to return to the scene, stroll or maybe take a Popemobile ride around the piazza, and inspect the chalk outline of the body. Would the *polizia* carefully trace the fine silk vestments, conical hat, and scepter still clutched as he hit the ground? Maybe old Italian women from the poorer quarters of Rome would come and make the spot a shrine that old Italian women from medieval hill towns would come visit a couple of Sundays a year. More likely, most of the country *nonne* would stay home and worship the local saints, but even if a few of them a week made the trip, I'd feel a little better knowing I'd given the old *goomads* something to do.

Then I'd return to my family's ancestral village, Prata del Principato Ultra, to see if the *paesani* there had reclaimed me as one of their own, if the local merchants had capitalized on me, by selling tourists to nearby Pompeii little paperweight and ash tray replicas of me standing triumphant astride the fallen Pope — bomb in my left hand, relic, maybe a vertebra of the Blessed Virgin's spine — in my right. I'd buy a few dozen of these and mail them to my mother. When they finally arrived at her house two months later, she'd find a way to work them into her curio display, between the Capodimonte women on horseback and the Lladro clowns. The ones she couldn't find a place for, she'd send to my aunts, whom she'd call.

"Yeah, my son killed the Pope. No, now they love him over there, the greaseballs."

My sister would glue one of the ashtrays to the dashboard of her car, beneath a dangling Italian *tricolore* made of beads. Stopped at a light, she would extinguish a cigarette in the folds of the prone pontiff's robe, set her radio to techno, and, all sunglasses and teeth, rev her engine.

As public approval of my blow for the repressed grew, my father would change his tune.

"You know, Son, it's not much of likeness," he'd say, holding one of the souvenir ashtrays in his hand, "but we're all very proud. Your mother wants me to carve a statue just like it for the front of the house."

This is because she is a good Italian mother who wants the world to know her son is a big man, even if she herself considers him a sacrilegious pain in the ass.

So I'd be sitting in my city apartment, the one my parents never visit, thinking that maybe I could have hurled the bomb away from the Pope or thinking that it was my bomb, after all. I would call my sister to ask if I should mention this second possibility to my mother, since it's the duty of any good Italian son to confess to his parents anything strange he might have done or might do, especially if that something is liable to cause trouble in the family, not to mention a stir in the world beyond.

"Delores, I'm starting to think I killed the Pope on purpose."

"I told you you were possessed."

"You think Mom would be pissed off if I told her?"

"She's gonna be pissed off over something. It might as well be a religious thing. At least it's not about your girlfriend."

As a good Italian girl, it's my sister's duty to monitor the parents' emotional tendencies and help the rest of us keep all family conflict in perspective. Ironically, it's also her job to oil the machinery of conflict and keep it working for, not against, us.

"So was it really an accident?" She'd ask.

"I hope so, but I'm not sure."

"See?"

We would agree that killing the Pope was a cry for help or attention. Never again in family conversation would I be, "Peter, your cousin the writer" or "Peter, your nephew who moves in with a new girl every month" or "Peter, Theresa's son, the *ciucc'* who never comes to funerals." Instead, now immortalized in souvenir, the fame of my name would endear me: "Cousin Peter Boy, the one who killed the Pope."

Killing the Pope would be my act of atonement. I would atone for "learning to be stupid in college," "living like a teenager," forgetting what my parents taught me. But I would also atone for all they haven't accomplished. My father has always wanted to take my mother to Italy, to the place their grandfathers told them about. And I have always told him they should go, even if that Italy is as dead as my Pope would be. It's just, my father always said, they couldn't get the cash together — all the assets tied up in figurines and statuary. But now, with the money gained from my fame, I would be able to send them, and send them in style.

In the months leading up to the trip, I could teach the whole family some basic Italian to supplement the dialect words we sprinkle into daily conversation. During one of our family lessons around my parents' gigantic, hand-carved dining room table, my father would raise his hand.

"Let me ask you, Son," he would pipe up, "I know it's not nice, but when I say 'a fissa 'e mamata,' what would I really be saying?"

"It means, 'Up your ass, Pattelli!'" my mother would blurt out from the kitchen, where, bored with the lesson, she would have gone to stir her sauce.

Most curses in Italian seem to mean "up your ass." Maybe I could teach them how to say, "Up the Pope's ass," "A fissa 'e Papa." That way they would have something to say to the Italian media who would interview them as i genitori, the parents, of l'assassino. My parents could explain to the Italian press, or maybe the Italian press could explain to my parents, why profanities are the only Italian words we remember.

Sometime in the early 1980s, just after the Pope had visited New York, we stood staring at the papal glam shot my father had bought from a Yankee Stadium vendor. My father was explaining that this Pope, even though he wasn't Italian and my father didn't like his personality, deserved respect. Why? Because he spoke seven languages, that's why. Standing there with us, an Irish friend, Mike Flanagan, asked what Italian my father could speak.

"Oh, Mike," Dad confessed, "only the bad words."

Which he promptly taught us, and which soon had Flanagan in stitches — Flanagan, who must have been thinking he'd caught a glimpse into the true Italian soul, or at least confirmed one of his father's stereotypes of the guineas.

So now, as i genitori dell'assassino, my parents would take a walking tour of Southern Italy and find out why our families left such a beautiful country in the first place. With Italian television cameras rolling, they would discover from distant cousins taking espresso in a one-horse piazza, that some Pope along the line had been responsible for the emigration; that someone in that

Pope's sub rosa employ had produced a specious document indicating that our ancestral lands had been long before secretly deeded to the Church, and that since our forebears couldn't gain an audience with the Pope or even one of his bishops, they had had no choice but to abandon the Italian ship and wait for the crew of an American steamer to pick them up, throw them in the hold, and put them to work on the New York skyline.

My parents would return home with a new perspective, one to share with all of us.

Their plane would touch down at Kennedy Airport late on a Thursday night. They would be tired but exhilarated by their journey, the sites, the demands of celebrity. I would wait by the baggage claim, a box of *pignoli* cookies for Dad in my left hand, a bouquet of white roses for Mom in my right. The picture of a good Italian son.

My father would approach, wrap me in a bear hug. His tears would dampen my collar.

"It's o. k., Son," he'd whisper, releasing me, and reaching for the white handkerchief in his back pocket.

Her hair done up in a red, white, and green kerchief, my mother would receive the bouquet like a dignitary. She would kiss me on both cheeks. Then she would step back, look me in the eye, walk forward again.

"Peter, do you believe in God?"

"Yes, Mom, I believe I do."

She would kiss me on the cheek again.

"In that case, we just want you to know: We got your point!"

RESURRECTING THE POPE

"Your son saw the Pope."

"The Pope's dead, Terry!"

My father answers my mother in the impatient tone he usually reserves for kyboshing the two-hour ride to her sister's house in Jersey.

My mother bites her lip and stares at the Our Lady of Peace Church calendar hanging next to the stove.

"He had a vision. He has visions. When he was little, he had an imaginary friend, Susie."

"That's different, Terry. Maybe this time he just had too much linguine with the clams before he turned in."

Most of the time my father believes that any Pope, especially this recently deceased Pope, is at least a little supernatural, but the idea of papal resurrection is too much for him. He and his friends prefer the Pope as metaphor.

"It's amazing, Charlie, the way he suffered."

"Like Christ."

"That's it!"

My father wants to believe me.

My mother does believe me, but doesn't want to.

This is because I am a first-born Italian son, whose word is family gospel, even if he has no idea what he's talking about and no one really likes his opinions.

The phone rings: my mother.

"How old are you now?" she wants to know.

"Thirty-seven."

"Are you sure? You'd forget your head if it wasn't attached."

"You were there."

"Christ was thirty-three when he came back."

"I'm not Christ, Mom. And if I come back, it'll be as a tree. And I didn't say I saw Christ. There's a small chance I might have seen the Pope."

"What? The Pope's not like Christ?"

"Just forget I told you. And please don't say anything."

The next day the phone rings: Cousin Johnny.

"Your mother tells me you saw the dead Pope."

He's already had two heart attacks, but I can hear him sucking on a cigarette, chuckling through a cough.

"I'm not surprised," he goes on, "you were always a sacrilegious asshole."

"You called to tell me that?"

"And to see if you wanted to play golf this Sunday?"

I can't believe any of this, except that I might have seen the Pope. Last Sunday, after days of worldwide anticipation, he finally, definitely died. Then, Monday morning, as a heavy rain was pounding the smudgy panes of my bedroom window, through half-sleep I heard a voice. I thought it was a voice, and I think it moaned, "Sympathy," or else, "Sin for me."

"What did the Pope say?" my mother asks as she dotes, all five feet, two inches of her serving me an outsized ceramic bowl of sea-green *lenticchie past'*, lentil and spinach soup with pasta, a childhood favorite.

I keep eating, watching my father, who sits at my parents' enormous dining room table, his head tilted back now, staring at the ceiling. He massages the bridge of his nose with thumb and forefinger.

"Please, Mom, forget it. It was probably a dream. Nothing."

As soon as my mother sets a bowl in front of him, my father looks down again, exhales, and lifts a weighty soupspoon. His usual expression of dining-room contentment returns. He raises his salt-and-pepper eyebrows and begins eating.

My mother returns to the kitchen, on a mission to keep the inevitable second helpings warm.

"Has she been on this all week?" I ask.

He rolls his eyes and keeps eating his legumes.

He doesn't come out and ask me about the Pope. Not yet. As a good Italian father, it's his duty to be skeptical of his only son, without hurting that son's feelings by making him think he could in any way be wrong.

He stops eating for a moment, closes his eyes, and announces, "I'm tying flies, Son. Trout season opens in five days."

As a ne'er-do-well intellectual, I'm usually available to fish with my father, often during the week. Most days I can sleep until ten or eleven in the morning, until the sun floods my bedroom and warms the futon mattress to the point where I sweat, lie in half-sleep, and begin to contemplate lunch. So when a diaphanous figure in a conical hat appeared at my bedside, I may have heard him say, "Food for me," or maybe "Fruit and tea." His accent was strong, so I can't be sure. I can't be sure I heard or saw anything, in fact, though knowing one way or the other would make me feel a lot better about mortality.

My mother arrives at the Our Lady of Peace Rectory, just as Monsignor Barò is cooking himself a hearty breakfast of sausage and eggs. A Broadway dancer in his twenties, at sixty-eight the monsignor weighs three hundred pounds, but retains a youthful shock of red hair. He and my parents grew up in the same Brooklyn neighborhood and wound up in the same suburb. My mother likes to visit Monsignor Barò, to reminisce about the old neighborhood and remind him of her younger brother's success. She was once responsible for rooting against Barò, when, throughout the 1960s, he and my uncle were rivals on the Brooklyn Diocese musical theater circuit. For years they appeared in many of the same productions, for the same audiences of aging Italian immigrants and their children, who believed more in homegrown, church-sponsored entertainment than in the church itself. Their rivalry lasted until both men realized they could never be lovers in such an environment and went their separate ways — Barò to Broadway, then seminary; my uncle to the opera, then cooking school. By reminding Barò of my uncle's success, my mother creates drama, the essence of Italian memory. She begins coolly.

"I saw the hair in the window and thought I'd drop in."

He flashes a broad smile. "You know you're always welcome, Theresa. Can I make you an omelet?"

Barò refers to my mother by her Christian name, reminding her of his status.

"No, thank you. I'm on my way to Anthony's restaurant."

"How's your brother doing?"

"He has more money than God, but he doesn't know how to spend it."

Barò grumbles, plates his breakfast, and invites my mother to sit.

"Money avails us nothing," he says with conviction, "if we're not settled in spirit."

"That's right. How are your sausage?"

"Perfect. Are you sure you wouldn't like some?"

"No. Anthony makes me the veal. It's out of this world."

He grimaces, then washes down a mouthful of sausage with a shot of espresso.

"So what's new?" he asks.

My mother waits until he lifts of forkful of omelet to his lips.

"My son saw the Pope."

The monsignor lowers his fork.

"What Pope? We're still waiting for the conclave. My guess is it'll be another week, at least. They're talking about a German."

"He saw the dead one. He had a vision."

Barò slides back from the table and takes a moment to weigh the tidings.

"Where did he see the Pope?"

"In his bedroom."

"Here?"

"No, in the city. He likes it there. . . . Father, what's the matter with my son?"

"Is he still a member of the church?"

"No. He went to college and had sex."

"Does he still consider himself a Catholic?"

"He goes with Jewish girls."

Barò strokes his chin and drums his fingers on the table.

"Theresa, do you know what this could mean to our parish?"

A day later the phone rings. My sister.

"Mommy's gonna ask you to have dinner with the priest."

"What priest?"

"The monsignor. The one with the red hair. The fag."

"The fag."

"What do you want from me? She thinks they're gonna make you a saint or something."

"Jesus Christ."

"Jesus Christ on the cross!" my father yells.

My mother has informed him that she's inviting the Monsignor to dinner.

"He talked to someone in Italy," she explains. "They want to see your son."

"C'mon, Terry, use your head."

Every other month my father confesses his major sins, except for the embarrassing ones, to a gentle Chinese prelate seated on the other side of a wooden screen. After Mass they shake hands. Once in a while, my father invites this foreign father to the local soft-serve shop for a "frappe." That's enough church for any grown Italian man, especially an old-fashioned Italian man, who suspects his monsignor is as queer as a three-dollar bill. At home, in the evening, my father likes to eat quietly, finger his rosary, then submit to the most powerful force in his life, cable television.

One night, feeling guilty for refusing to feed the monsignor, my father scans his hundred and fifty channels of bliss for Catholic programming. He sits through two-thirds of *King of Kings* and a documentary on the papal selection process. It's nearly two a. m., but he still can't sleep. Thoughts of eternal damnation. *Agita* from my mother's steak *pizzaiol'*. Changing the channel one last time, he is just about to nod off, when an elderly pontiff and his attendants suddenly fill the screen. The high clerics are seated in a ballroom. Processional music plays. The priests are watching a fashion show, a parade of models in ecclesiastical vestments: silk and chiffon albs, velvet fanons, embroidered chasubles, neon miters. Like the long-suffering and recently departed Pope, my father drifts in and out of consciousness.

He wakes up shivering as the sun begins to rise. My mother has stayed up all night to wait for her thirty-year-old daughter, still living alone in the basement apartment, to come home from a date. The coffee is made. She sits at the dining room table, buttering enough hunks of toasted Italian bread to feed twenty people. She drops the knife when my father stumbles in and practically shouts, "All right, Terry, call the priest!"

"I had a vision," my father claims, laying his hand on mine. He nods slowly, his eyes welling up. "Ah, Merciful Lord!"

He blows his nose and gathers himself, then squeezes my shoulder.

"Let me ask you, Son. What did the Pope do in your vision?

My mother answers from the kitchen, where she's making sweet dough for a special batch of sacerdotal *struffoli*.

"He came to his bedroom and kicked out that little bitch girlfriend of his."

A retired cop, my father continues the line of questioning.

"What did he say, Son?"

"I don't know, Dad. I think he wanted something to eat."

This time my mother pokes her head around the corner.

"They all do," she insists, "because they can't have sex."

"I think I saw the Pope," my father confesses, "and his whole, ah, what do you call them. . . ?"

"Nuncios? Archbishops?" I guess.

"Tell you the truth, I think it was the whole College of Cardinals."

One of the few terms my father recalls from the cable documentary, the term brings a smile to his ruddy face.

"What were they doing?" I ask.

"You're gonna think your father's crazy, but they were watching a fashion show."

"You know, Dad, that sounds familiar. I think it's a movie. Yeah, it's Fellini. *Roma*. Were you watching t. v. last night?"

"Fellini?"

"Fellini."

"He was Italian?"

"Fellini, Dad. He was Roman."

"You see. It's a sign. The Romans know."

The next day the phone rings. My parents, each of them on a separate cordless receiver.

"Hello, Son."

They must be sitting too close together. A blast of feedback. My father drops his handset.

"A *managgia diavolo*," I hear him say as he bends to pick it up. "Son, your mother has something to tell you."

When an Italian husband has his wife close at hand, he automatically defers to her in all surprise announcements. This is generally a function of laziness and of fear he'll say something that might start trouble.

My mother shouts, like a radio announcer giving away a prize: "You're gonna be the next Pope!"

My parents can no longer ignore the obvious messages from above. They've decided that the dead Pope wants me to succeed him, and is calling on them to prepare the way.

"I'm not even a priest," I protest.

"Neither was Saint Peter, Son."

"He was crucified."

"But he wasn't a priest."

"I'm also not celibate."

My mother is undaunted. While awaiting her own vision, she has apparently been boning up on papal history.

"One Pope fathered seven children while he was a cardinal," she says. "Did you know that, Mr. PhD? So have your fun now, while no one's watching."

A good Italian patriarch, my father reminds me of my responsibilities in the most generic of terms.

"That's right, son. Pretty soon you'll have to buckle down and put your nose to the grindstone."

A good Italian matriarch, my mother punctuates her husband's sentence.

"Nothing good comes easy."

"We'll do the work on our end," my father reassures me. "Just get yourself geared up."

"To be the Pope? What are you asking me?"

"Monsignor says it's at least sixty-forty. All you have to do for now," my mother says, "is think about a name."

"Oh, Son, your mother was reading up on some very nice names last night. What do you think about Bonifacio?"

At home that evening I sit at the cherry wood desk my great-grandfather hand carved in Brooklyn with tools carried in 1906 from a workshop in his tiny Mezzogiorno hill town. What else can I do but respect my family's wishes? I search the desk drawers for my childhood crucifix. I find it buried beneath a stack of yellowed college term papers, shrouded in the pages of a decade-old women's lingerie catalog. This crucifix features a removable Christ. Actually, the avatar is mounted on a rectangular piece of wood that slides upward to reveal a secret compartment designed to hold a votive taper. One of Catholicism's many mysteries. During my teenage years, I often used the compartment to hide the instruments of sin – condoms, joints and pornography – in plain sight.

I place the crucifix on my desk and scour my bookshelves for a coffee-table tome called *The Lives of the Popes,* inherited from a great-aunt by way of my mother, who told me to keep it "as a collector's item." I find it between *The Bhagavad-Gita* and Machiavelli's *Prince.* Setting it down on the desk, next to the crucifix, staring at the two talismans, I try to remember how to say an "Our Father."

As I scan the table of contents, I'm drawn first to the papal name Sylvester. But then it sounds a little too slick and sinister, and Sylvester III, I discover, was excommunicated, exiled, and is listed among the antipopes. I'm not even sure what an antipope is.

I can see this is going to take a little while, so I change into my silk robe, make myself a pot of coffee, and begin weeding out the undesirables.

Pius XII, the Pope of my father's youth, tolerated the Holocaust.

Pius IX was exiled during the European revolutions of 1848, led in Italy by the great Garibaldi. He later forbade all Catholics from participating in Italian politics. During the First Vatican Council in 1870, he answered growing challenges to his authority by simply having himself and all future Popes declared infallible, then imprisoning himself in Vatican City for the remainder of his life.

Leo XII restricted the sale of wine in taverns.

Leo V, like most Popes, came to power through a political compromise, then was deposed and assassinated.

Clement XIV died of depression brought on by fear of poisoning at the hands of the Jesuits.

Clement VII's weak policies led to the most recent sack of Rome.

Benedict VI was strangled by a priest while imprisoned in Castel Sant' Angelo.

Benedict XIII allowed an extortionist to make and carry out Vatican policy.

Benedict IX had to contend with five other purported Popes during his oft-interrupted tenure.

Alexander VIII had once been Grand Inquisitor.

Alexander VI indeed fathered seven children while a cardinal, and two more while Pope. (I might keep his name in the running.)

Sixtus V ordered countless public executions, in the name of civic order.

Gregory XIII supported Queen Elizabeth I of England.

John XI's papacy was dominated by his mother, who had had the preceding Pope deposed and murdered.

John XXI was killed when the ceiling above his bed collapsed.

John VIII was the first Pope to be assassinated.

Urban VI became paranoiacally deranged by his election.

Urban II launched the First Crusade.

Lucius II was killed in battle with insurgent Roman citizens.

Gelasius was imprisoned by Roman aristocrats.

Gregory I was responsible for Gregorian chants.

A Holy Roman Emperor mutilated an antipope on Gregory V's behalf.

Gregory VII, like a few recent American Presidents, claimed the right to depose all princes and to have all Christians as his subjects.

To expiate his ecclesiastical peccadillos, Stephen VI had the corpse of the previous Pope exhumed, put on trial, mutilated, and thrown into the Tiber River. He was later deposed and strangled in prison.

All of these are off the list, but a lot remain.

My father's suggestion, Bonifacio, Boniface, seems all right. Boniface VIII once sent a note to the King of France, beginning, "Listen, Son. . . .," so I can understand my prototypical dad's attachment to the name. But I want to be somewhat original, and we've already had *troppi Bonifaci,* too many Popes named Boniface. I nix it.

Next I eliminate the names that I just don't like. That takes care of Eugene, Felix, Nicholas, Paul, and Theodore.

Then I consider the current church scandals, which leads me to discard any name with a homosexual ring. Out go Celestine, Fabian, Gaius, Marius, Paschal, Sisinnius, and Valentine.

Still many possibilities.

I want to be a Pope of peace, so I rule out any name that sounds too military or too Roman. Goodbye to Victor and to any remaining name ending in -us, -as or -es. I'm particularly sorry to lose Anacletus, Cletus, Simplicimus and Zozimus, but what can you do?

Because I am fundamentally happy to be alive, I discount the name of any Pope who lasted less than five years' time in the Holy See. So fall Agatho, Conon, Lando, Pontian, and Sabinian.

I have narrowed the field to three: Constantine, Soter, and Vitalian. Soter and Vitalian are both saints, which can only improve my image among family members. Constantine is a strong, attractive name, and the eighth-century Pope who took it was North African: a bonus in the current political climate. Unfortunately, Constantine intrigued with the Byzantine Emperor and Exarch of Ravenna, whose policies caused rioting and bloodshed in the streets of Rome, on Constantine's watch. This poor bit of judgment and the three years of general famine that followed Constantine's consecration led me next to Soter.

Soter was one of the earliest Popes, so has the advantage of relative anonymity. He barely exists in the annals of history. But since my self-esteem isn't quite that low, I move on to Vitalian.

Like most of my male ancestors, Vitalian was both a native of Campania and a mild-mannered man. His gentle eloquence convinced the estranged Byzantine Emperor Constans to visit Rome. The problem for Vitalian was that Constans apparently had no respect. He sacked a string of cities on his way, and, o. k., some were barbarian strongholds, but that still doesn't excuse his behavior. In Rome itself he made nice with the Pope and his officials during public ceremonies, but then stole the bronze tiles from the roofs of many Roman buildings, including the Pantheon. My father, also a construction foreman by training, would be very disappointed.

So there at my cherry wood desk I sit, bereft of tradition. I look around the room for a sign. I spot photos of my niece Ashleigh and nephew Tyler above my desk. And suddenly, all becomes clear. I will need a name that reflects my historical significance as the first American Pope.

Monsignor Barò comes to Friday dinner at my parents': an *antipast'* of *gabinadin'*, pickled eggplant salad, then stuffed *calamad'* over capellini, followed by my mother's mountain of *struffoli*, those little honey-covered dough balls no one but older Italians likes. Barò is overwhelmed.

"Delicious, Theresa," he announces, wiping the corners of his mouth with one of my parents' only-for-holidays napkins. "If I knew back in Brooklyn you could cook like this, I would've married you before Pasquale had the chance."

"Oh, Father, stop!"

My mother blushes and runs to the kitchen. She returns seconds later with another stuffed *calamad'* skewered on the end of a barbecue fork.

The monsignor raises his glass, looks to both of my parents, and says jovially, "I'd like to propose a trip to Rome. The two of you, me, our bishop, and a good *Napolitan'* lawyer." My father stops chewing, looks down, and for a moment says nothing. Then, thinking perhaps of Sofia Loren, Anna Magnani, and hunks of genuine pork *soprasatt'*, he smiles.

"Would it be like a tour, Father?" He asks.

"Like a guided tour," Barò assures him. "The bishop goes at least once a year. He knows all the best places to eat."

Still wielding the impaled squid, my mother interrupts. "But it's all Italian food, right?"

"Of course, Theresa. The best in the world."

She frowns.

"What's wrong?"

"You don't like my food?"

Seeking to maintain the family's *bella figura* at all costs, my father intercedes.

"No, Terry, Monsignor's just saying we'll go top shelf. And you'll get a break from cooking."

First my mother looks anxious, lost; then her face softens.

"Does the bishop know where the *Three Coins in the Fountain* fountain is?" She asks.

"Of course. And we'll stay in a fabulous hotel right near Vatican City. Lots of shopping. A beautiful part of town."

My mother is momentarily mollified, so my father, doing his duty as a good Italian husband, asks a question to fill her uncharacteristic silence.

"Let me ask you, Father. Why do we need the lawyer?"

"Oh, just a formality. He'll argue for your son's election."

My mother brings two histories of the papacy to read on the plane. She slips another into my father's suitcase. The papal conclave is already underway when they arrive. Denied an audience with the assembled College, the bishop has his lawyer finagle a meeting with the Vatican's Director of Public Relations. The lawyer tells the Director the story of our family's visions, arguing that a mystically anointed Pope would be good for business. The Director warns that competition will be stiff.

"There's talk of a South American, even an African," he explains. "And of course the Italians prefer to return the title to the family."

The lawyer only raises an eyebrow.

"*Ma*," the Director continues, "*vediamo un po'*. Maybe we can work something out."

The lawyer carries the hopeful news back to my mother and to the monsignor, who is ready with a backup plan. He has the counselor call the Italian press. The next day the story of our visions is headline news. The leader of the left-wing minority in Parliament calls the visions a sham. The right-wing Prime Minister accuses him of anti-Americanism. The parliamentary session degenerates into a maelstrom of accusations and epithets. Officials and prominent journalists demand the unprecedented interruption of the conclave. Around the world clerics appear on camera, arguing for the separation of state from church.

Worried and embarrassed by the attention that the monsignor is drawing to my cause, my parents hunker down in their hotel room, to learn more about the institution to which they plan to sacrifice their only son. There they sip complimentary *spumante* and read from their growing papal library.

"Who knew Pius XII was a Nazi?" My father remarks, while reading the book my mother has assigned him.

"Of course he was, Pattelli," she answers, flaunting her new command. "He was Bavarian nuncio. The Germans loved him."

Recalling the hundreds of hours of World War II documentaries he's watched, my father adds, "Like I always tell the kids, Terry, watch out for the Germans."

One evening, as he escorts my mother down the Corso Vittorio Emanuele, my father senses they are being followed. Without warning he pulls open the *portone* of a sixteenth-century *palazzo*, and hurries my mother into the vestibule. She is all ready for an argument, but when she turns and sees his eyes fixed on the door, his jaw clenched, she keeps her mouth shut and moves closer. They return to their hotel, and report the incident to their lawyer.

"Agents, probably harmless," he reassures them. "Some people in Vatican City just like to know who their challengers are."

That week, accompanied by armed bodyguards, my parents appear on several Italian talk shows, on networks owned by the Prime Minister. To a string of hosts, they explain through a translator that the Pope came back to anoint their son, because he was a historic Pope and could do things like that, like the one who made himself infallible.

"Why did the Americans see him as such a great Pope?" one host asks.

His entire repertoire of Italian hand gestures on full display, my father attempts to answer. "He had a certain something, like . . ."

"Like Frank Sinatra," my mother breaks in. "The first time we saw Sinatra, we thought, 'Who is this skinny crooner?' The first time we saw the Pope, God rest his soul, we thought, 'Who is this Polack with all the energy?'"

"And we liked his message," my father says, before my mother continues.

"That's right. He said exactly what we tell our kids. Don't think you're safe just because you're using those condoms, and priests shouldn't have sex."

Fearing that the media might actually begin to evaluate the policies of "Humanae Vitae"'s defunct champion, and having seen my mother in action, the Vatican blinks. By the end of the week, my parents, the monsignor, the bishop and the lawyer have their audience. Two days later Delores and I are flown into Roma Fiumicino, where we are greeted by a beaming Monsignor Barò, who in the cab to our luxury hotel room, hands me an address for the tailor who will make my vestments. The following Monday the Vatican calls a press conference inside the Sistine Chapel.

Delores and I stand in the hallway outside, awaiting my dramatic entrance.

"What are you gonna do first?" She asks.

"I don't know. I could re-learn the Mass. And I'm a writer. I could write encyclicals and bulls. And I've always wanted to live in Rome."

Delores is violently chewing a handful of honey-roasted almonds.

"I don't know. Not me. It's so humid here."

She fans herself.

"But, remember, you can do it for a while, and if you don't like it, you quit."

We turn to watch the monitor above our heads. A minute later our parents appear in front of the microphones. Flashbulbs pop. Reporters are yelling at them in twenty-five different languages. My father, a foot taller than my mother, has on his cop face: taut, expressionless, eyes surveying the room. He approaches the dais.

"My wife," he says flatly, "has an announcement to make."

"Did you at least pick a name?" Delores asks me.

I nod. "I have it down to either Jared or Todd."

I imagine myself regal in a flowing surplice, doing the pontifical hand wave, blessing a hundred thousand worshippers in Saint Peter's Square. Or sitting in one of the Borgia apartments, my feet up on a gold-stitched hassock, the picture of comfort in my silk bedclothes, ready to accept a late night glass of San Giovese from my butler, as I read through the itinerary for my goodwill trip to a tropical country with millions of impoverished Catholics and great beaches. I think of the endless possibilities for nepotism. I can make a bishop of my cousin Alphonso, a house-bound neurotic and burden to his ailing old father. I can appoint my meddling Aunt Mary as Special Counsel to the Archbishop of Atlanta, a place I've never liked. And if there is no Archbishop of Atlanta, I can create one. I can even settle my parents' eternal, mutual grudges against their in-laws, by beatifying both of my grandmothers.

"Quiet down, everybody," my mother pleads. "Quiet, please. I want to announce to you all that the College of Cardinals wants my son Peter to be the next Pope."

The assembled media cheer.

"But they prefer a different a name."

"So do we," my sister cracks.

"So," my mother continues, "they said he could use his middle one, since it's Latinate. So he would be Pope Mario I."

As an Italian *American*, maybe I can insist on Pope Mario Jared or Jared Mario or Mario Todd. Maybe I can ask to be called by just one name at a time. Or maybe no one will call me anything but "Your Holiness" ever again.

My sister interrupts my reverie with a hug and pulls out her cell phone, to text her entire contacts list.

I settle into contemplation. I will have a life entirely different from the one I've imagined. Maybe this is what the last Pope went through. One minute he was an actor in Krakow, the next he was riding through the Eternal City in a bullet-proof car, wearing spectacular hats. Larger forces, my parents, are prevailing. Then I see that my father isn't smiling. Neither is my mother, who remains at the microphone, waiting for the applause to die. When it does, she clears her throat.

"Now, God bless the cardinals for their choice," she says, but there's a problem."

The crowd freezes.

"They're making a very generous offer, and we appreciate the gesture. But they can keep the job."

A collective gasp. Monsignor Barò's jowls collapse.

My mother's eyes study the heavenly humanity of the ceiling — the Creation, Adam and Eve Sent Out of Eden, the Tribulations of the Damned — then settle on the crowd, the cardinals, the camera, and seem through the monitor to be looking right at me.

"My Peter Boy thinks he's a man of the world, but if he came over here and tried to run this place by himself, in the name of all that's holy, you'd ruin him."

The room erupts in laughter and catcalls. My mother turns to my father, who puts an arm around her. Then the couple who gave me life make the sign of the cross in unison, and shuffle off the screen.

Peter looked to the heavens.

"You've gotta be kidding."

Evelyn stood in front of him, feeling as though the headache she knew was coming had already arrived.

"Can you just listen? I'm not saying you have to go to church . . . No . . . yes, I am saying that, but you only have to go for a little while, through the Pre-Cana. That's it."

"But why? I haven't gone to Mass in God-knows-how-long. If I went back now, they'd probably excommunicate me."

So dramatic.

"Look," Evelyn said calmly, "I'm sure it'll be fine. You only had a civil marriage, right? And all the Pope business was over and done with a while ago."

So beautiful and so reasonable.

"I just want to get married in the Church," she told him, then kissed his forehead. "It feels right, you know, with you."

He nodded.

"And it'll make my mother — both of our mothers — very happy. That's important to me."

He rolled his eyes.

The mothers, the Italian women.

"They need the ceremony," he answered, meaning, "you do too."

Evelyn smiled.

"So we're lying to the priest."

She knew how Peter loved the concept of scruples.

"Not lying to him," Evelyn answered. "We're just telling him you're going back to the Church. Which you are. And who knows? You may like it."

"Donkeys," he said, grinning, "when they fly." He turned to his bride-to-be. "O. K. How do we start this?"

Evelyn beamed for a glorious moment, then grabbed Peter by the button-down shirt, undid the top button, pulled the shirt over his head, and shoved him backwards, onto the leather couch they'd inherited from his mother a few months before.

A week later they were sitting on the old couch after dinner, drinking sweet red wine and, as each knew the other liked to do, rehearsing their past and future together. This was how they kept track of desires and reminded themselves how at the center of these desires dwelled a mutual aching need for mid-life intimacy, the connection they'd been denied for twenty years spent in misfit lovers' arms.

Peter leaned across the couch and whispered in Evelyn's ear.

She tucked her chin and blushed just enough for him to infer the privilege she must have felt, that they were here, now, together, and not, thank God, living separately in a monastery and convent somewhere in fourteenth-century Italy, where they'd have been close enough to see each other picking berries on a wooded path but able to communicate only by blinking their eyes, stealing now and then gentle caresses behind dense copses, where they would have to rendezvous, knowing full well that they could at any moment be discovered by a mother superior or a wild boar.

"I love you too," she told him.

He drew back to his end of the couch, satisfied.

"So when's the Pre-Cana start?"

"It doesn't."

He sat waiting for the punchline, but Evelyn only frowned.

"We're not getting married in the church."

"What?"

"I had a fight with my mother."

"But you said she'd be happy."

"I never got a chance to tell her."

At that moment Peter fully understood why Italians worshipped the Madonna. Woman was faith incarnate, pure mystery.

The previous day Evelyn had called Rose Ann, her mother, to break the news.

"Mom, guess what? Peter and I were talking, and we decided we're gonna get married."

A brief silence.

"Well, I hope you're planning to get married in the church! Last time you didn't, and look what happened! That other boy fell to doing drugs, and you never made it to the altar."

Evelyn could feel her face twitch. She loved her mother, missed being with her, but at this distance, and with a plan in the works, talking to her could be like watching your least favorite movie scene for the hundredth time. Rose Ann had made Evelyn strong, but sometimes too strong for her own taste. All those dates with boys that her mother had told her she couldn't go on. All those trips to friends in other cities that she didn't want Evelyn to take. Strangers were dangers. Any place outside their Tampa neighborhood could be a pitfall. Times like now Evelyn just wanted to scream. Instead she replied in an eerily calm voice, as if a higher power were speaking through her.

"You know what, mother? No church. That's it. We're getting married in a tree."

The words just came to her.

"A tree? What's that supposed to mean?"

"I don't know, mother. Have a nice day."

Click.

Peter was baffled.

"A higher power?"

"Yeah."

"Not just your mother pissed you off?"

Sure. But how could she let her mother have the final say or accentuate the negative. Evelyn looked at the ceiling, trying to ease the tension now tightening her neck and shoulders; then, like a woman possessed, she rolled her head around and around, puffing out through her nose at every rotation. Finally, her heart-shaped face returned to rest, her eyes remaining closed. She imagined herself and her mother racing each other up the nave of a Gothic cathedral, each carrying a different color bouquet of flowers meant for the single empty crystal vase waiting on the altar.

"Can we talk about this later?" She asked Peter. "I need a few days to recover."

The next day the phone rang: Rose Ann.

"I hate to tell you," she began in her Florida Italian American drawl, "but when you do come back to your senses about church, they're gonna make it awfully hard on that boy to marry you."

"Mom, you're giving me a migraine." Evelyn rubbed her forehead. "Why are you worried about the church? You're not even really religious."

She heard a gasp on the other end of the line, followed by deep hum, like a Buddhist incantation.

"How can you say that?" Rose Ann growled, in her highest dudgeon. "I'm a devout Catholic. Every other Sunday I go to late Mass with your Aunt Bernice at Our Lady of Perfect Holiness. And when it's over we always talk to Father Scanlon."

Evelyn waited for the dramatic pause.

"I am a VE-RY IM-POR-TANT MEM-BER OF THAT PAR-ISH. . . . And I'll tell you this, Honey: No church wedding, I ain't comin'."

Evelyn could hang up on her mother now, but she couldn't hang up forever. So she let the higher power speak again, and trusted the outcome to a literal interpretation of the message.

"Mother, I'll tell you what. Why don't you call Peter's mother? If the two of you can get the Pope to do a private ceremony, we'll get married in the Church."

Another pause.

"Well, Dear," Rose Ann said in a near whisper, "if that's what'll make you happy, you know I'll try."

"Oh, Mom. . . ."

Evelyn heard the sound of shuffling feet on her mother's end.

"Now, that's your Aunt Tabitha at the door. We'll talk later about the plans, Honey. Love you. Bye."

"So what'd she say?" Peter asked in that short New York way he could have.

How many times, Evelyn wondered, would she have to go back and forth, negotiating with her mother, explaining it all? And then explaining the explanation to Peter? She was forty years old and finally was marrying a man she wanted to marry *and should marry*. What else mattered? Evelyn flopped back on the couch and exhaled, her eyes registering nothing Peter could read, while her mind began planning their elopement.

The next sunny afternoon, Rose Ann flew around her Tampa ranch house like a trapped sparrow, twittering under her breath, thinking half-aloud about Peter's mother, the big woman — God love her — with the rosy cheeks, chestnut hair, and face that said to Rose Ann, "Get outta my way, Sugar, I'm comin' through." It was better to be on the same side as a woman like that, like her own *Nanna* Annalise. That woman, her *nanna,* was so tough that she once chased a Cuban neighbor, Daisy Rigofredo, down the block with a metal soup ladle, just because the woman winked at her husband as she walked past the front of their little house in Ybor City. She needed only to phone up this little reincarnation. If anyone would have had answers to all this marriage business, it would be *Nanna.* Maybe Theresa had them too.

"What do you mean they're not getting married in church?"

Theresa's voice crackled with a fire that made Rose Ann feel she was fully alive. Sixty-five years young and still kickin' like a mule.

"Who even knew they were getting married?"

"Well then, Theresa, I'm glad I called. It isn't right."

"That's right it's not right. . . . My son, the professor. He always has something to prove. Now he's gonna get married his way, just to spite us."

Rose Ann held the phone out in front of her for a moment, and drew a deep breath.

"Well, I do hope he's marrying Evelyn for a good reason."

"Of course he is. She's a beautiful girl. You should be very proud. But my son doesn't think. Did he tell you why he doesn't want to get married in church?"

It struck Rose Ann that the more she kept Theresa in the dark, the faster this little train would take her to Actionville, U. S. A.

"Well, I really can't imagine."

"Did he tell you he almost got me to make him the Pope?"

"I had heard him say something, but I thought, you know, it was one of his little jokes."

Rose Ann forced a laugh, which seemed to spur Theresa right in her saggy parts.

"Yeah? He's a real comedian, my precious son. I went through hell, and for nothing. He's still working in the city. . . . Did he tell you we went to

Rome and met the cardinals?"

"Why, no, but isn't that fascinating?"

Theresa liked the way Rose Ann's voice held on to the "g" in "-ing" words, like she was ringing a bell, like her dead aunts and uncles used to do — different accent, but still. Her voice softened.

"Yes, it was very interesting."

"Do you know a lot of those folks over there? Cardinals and such?"

"Of course. We met them all."

Theresa's mind drifted back toward anger.

"My son thought he had visions of the Pope. Did he tell you that?"

"Why, no, he never mentioned visions, but that sure is somethin'."

"He gets it from his father's family. They're all wack-a-do's."

"Wack-a-whats?"

"They're all crazy, because they're inbred. Peter Boy's grandmother and grandfather were first cousins."

Rose Ann again held the phone in front of her, her mouth hanging open, concern for her daughter and unborn grandchildren hardening her face into a mask of worry that almost but not quite overcame her desire to see Evelyn — who with all her mind-changing about men might be already too late to give birth — settled down once and for all. Rose Ann fell into a brief, silent trance.

"Are you there?"

Theresa's voice shot from the receiver like a rubber bullet. Rose Ann fumbled the phone, finally got hold of it, and lifted it slowly to her ear again.

"Yes, yes, I am, Theresa. I was just a little surprised is all."

"Don't worry. My son's not really crazy. He's just stupid."

Rose Ann spotted an opening.

"Well, you know, they all are sometimes. Men, I mean."

"Of course they are. With them running the world, it's amazing we're not all dead."

"Amen to that."

"My son's lucky I stopped the whole thing, or they would've eaten him alive over there."

Rose Ann heard the sound of a crinkling candy wrapper on Theresa's end.

"So if my son and your daughter don't want to get married in church,"

Theresa said, her words thick with chewing, "what can we do? I tell him I don't like to get involved in his love life."

"I tell Evelyn the same thing."

"So what can we do?"

Rose Ann lowered her voice a full octave and thirty decibels.

"Well, Theresa, maybe now that we're talkin' about it. . . ."

††
†

"I must be personal but ubiquitous," the Pope declared.

Guglielmo and Marcello stood at his side, scrawling notes on the blank pages of velveteen-covered journals issued to them for this purpose.

"It must be papal cabaret on a global scale."

The young pages looked up from their books, exchanging quizzical glances. Marcello, a wiry, energetic fellow and the senior page, spoke up.

"But, Your Eminence, we've already booked the *stadia*. These are the sorts of venues where His Holiness, your predecessor, made his mark as a pontiff of the people."

Hunched forward in his gilded wing chair, the Pope mumbled, his fingertips scraping the scruff of his creased pink neck.

"How do you know?" he snapped. "Where were *you* when my esteemed forebear was sufficiently ambulatory and adequately energetic to play stadium shows? I suppose when you were running around in your diapers, one fateful day you stopped before the television screen that was itself larger than you, and you watched our erstwhile Vicar of Christ as he married hundreds of couples in one fell swoop, and at that precious moment your infantile mind judged that he had left his indelible imprint on this office. Have you forgotten that shortly thereafter the people shot him down in the street?"

Just one person, Marcello thought, but held his tongue.

The Pope stood up, removed his house robe, threw it on a green leather fainting couch, and walked over to a full-length triptych mirror, where he stood in his boxer shorts and ankle-height black socks, flexing his pale, pendant pectorals, and turning sideways now and then to study the contour of his beanbag paunch. The truth was obvious: He had let himself go to pot. So many years he had worked tirelessly behind the scenes, laying the ground-work for this job, that he had foregone sessions in the Vatican gymnasium in favor of closed-door confabulations with his former Grace and mentor. He had emerged from those years with not only an uncanny knack for public proclamation and action, but also, in spite of his freakishly efficient metab-olism, a flabby midsection and toneless thighs. Without doubt he still cut a dashing figure in vestments, but he had lost the subtle swagger arising from a positive self-image, the pith of élan any good Pope needs to bestow credible benedictions. He could now, on occasion, appear to lack ummph.

If the Pope was embarrassed by his aging body, he seemed so neither to Guglielmo nor to Marcello, both of whom wished he would undress more discreetly, behind a screen.

"Your Eminence," Marcello began, hating, as always, to interrupt whatever thoughts could be occupying the old man's brain, while, like an exotic dancer-in-training, the pontiff undulated his bare abdomen before the mirror.

"Your Eminence," Marcello repeated.

"Yes, my sons?" the distracted Pope answered, his face registering some shame, now that he, like Adam, was feeling conscious of his nakedness but without at least the reassurance of the First Man's presumably exquisite physique.

"Your Grace, will you at least consider one large ceremony in a place where the masses are likely to feel an organic connection to the Church? Say, for argument's sake, in Bolivia?"

Any trace of benignity disappeared from the Pope's face.

"That's ludicrous!"

"What do you mean, Your Holiness?"

"I mean they worship mountains there, and the Earth Mother. Nothing could be more inimical to organic faith in our doctrine. In spite of Opus Dei's strength in that country, I've personally always believed that their in-nate love for ritual and metallic *objet d'art* are all that keep those people with us. No, Marcello, from this conviction I shall not be moved: Our fate is in the hands of the public relations people. It is imperative that we carefully manage events, especially in light of the entire Muslim debacle. A stadium full of people presents — not to sound overly scientific — too many variables. Can you imagine my presiding over not only marriages involving possibly hundreds of irrational brides, but also their extended families and putative well-wishers, who might themselves include any number of Islamofascists, indifferent Buddhists, God-less pagans or non-denominated lunatics? We would doubtless be compared with Moonies. And while I find the Reverend personally charming and a peerless connoisseur of oriental seafood, I must recognize the differences between our core constituencies, and act accordingly. Which, I believe, means returning to the power of clerical stardom. Don't you recall, Guglielmo, how it felt to speak with the priest of your village after Mass?"

"To speak honestly, Your Eminence, he frightened me."

"So long as he wasn't involved with all this dirty laundry we've been airing, I must assume that, although you feared him, you also yearned for his approval. Isn't it so?"

"Yes, I suppose . . ."

"Precisely. This is exactly why we must return to the most fundamental method of striking awe: staged intimacy with the divine. I marry one couple per ceremony, and that couple is assuredly ours for life. Imagine, if you will, the images of hysterical young girls' faces as they watch the performances of popular music stars. Today these young men seem mere screamers with lion manes for hair. They stuff themselves into snug pants and jump around as though their shoes were aflame. In my day the model of this type was Elvis Presley. When I perform an intimate ceremony before the cameras and the media throng, I may imagine that I am the King of Rock and Roll; my perspiration-soaked towel, a marriage vow; and my adoring fans, an attractive young couple glowing with love and submission to the mysterious sanction that only I may grant. Could there be a more magical moment? More compelling television? For you young people, it would be perhaps 'The Pope Unplugged.'"

The attendants exchanged looks of concession, and nodded. Marcello closed his journal and slipped his platinum pen behind his ear, thinking that if he should, after all, have to sit through hundreds of these individual matrimonies, he must at least make certain they would take place in theaters and clubs that stocked his favorite *digestivo*.

†††
†

Theresa was frustrated. She liked her religious things out. Especially around the holidays. Especially when company was coming.

"Where's the Infant of Prague, Pattelli?" she yelled from the bedroom, when she heard her husband's slow footfalls, his moans and groans as he made his slow way up the stairs and down the hallway. Finally, his face appeared at the door, concern knitting his brow.

"The Infant of Prague," she repeated.

"What, Theresa?"

"The statue. The one that's supposed to be in the corner. Where'd you put it?"

Pasquale mumbled under his breath.

"What's your problem, Pasquale? We're having company. He should be out."

"I don't know, Terry. Maybe the kids."

"Go scratch your ass. What kids? You're the only one up here. Were you cleaning again?"

Theresa said this as though accusing her husband of furtive masturbation.

"We need to change his suit," she went on.

"What suit?"

"The clothes. There's clothes for every season. Christmas, he wears the red suit. Where are you hiding it?"

Pasquale remembered the figure now: He wore a huge crown. With one outstetched hand he gave a benediction, while in the other hand he held a gold ball with a cross on top of it.

"How would you even get clothes on him?"

Theresa flung pairs of old underwear from an outsized plastic bin shoved in a corner next to her dresser.

"Don't play *faccia dost'*. You remember the clothes. They should be with the statue. I hope you didn't put him in your garage."

"Maybe, Theresa. I don't know. . . . Who's coming over?"

"The mother."

Pasquale spun the mental rolodex of all the mothers they knew.

"Mrs. Smithson?" he asked.

"No."

He sat down on the edge of the bed.

"Mrs. Fung."

"Not Fung. The mother. Evelyn's mother."

"I thought she lived in Florida."

"Of course she lives in Florida. She's coming up for the holidays."

Pasquale took a moment to decide that he liked the idea. The more company, the more food, the better. And they'd met the mother once before. A beautiful woman for her age.

"Oh, that's great. When did she decide this?"

"Two days ago."

"Very nice."

"Yeah. Then after Christmas she and I are leaving for Italy."

"What?"

"We're taking a flight to Rome on the twenty-sixth."

"What for?"

"We're going to see the Pope."

Pasquale frowned.

"What? Again?"

He imagined himself sitting in endless airport traffic the day after Christmas, cursing other drivers who'd be cursing back at him, giving him the Italian salute or whatever salute they used in their countries, with the windows rolled up. Then he imagined his wife knocking on the door of the Pope's apartment.

"Give the old man some peace, Terry."

Nothing good could come of this.

"Remember," he reminded his wife, "just when your son was set to be the Pope, you pulled him out. God doesn't like that."

"How do you know what God likes, Pattelli? If you can't help me, go out to your shop."

Pasquale was upset now. He didn't like being in his wife's doghouse, especially when it came to the Baby Jesus, or whatever the Infant of Prague was supposed to be. He stood up and headed downstairs to the computer room, hoping the machine was already on.

God must have been watching over him, because when he hit the space bar on the keyboard, the screen lit up, and the Internet program was open. Now, where were you supposed to type "Infant of Prague"? His daughter had explained it to him, but that was late at night, during a John Wayne movie. He remembered something about a white box. He found it and typed the term, hoping he'd spelled "Prague" right.

When he hit the return key, the program told him he had over 643,000 results. He decided to stick with the first twenty. Ten of those were for travel agencies that specialized in trips to Eastern Europe. A few more were Web sites for new parents. But a few looked good. He clicked on the first.

It surprised Pasquale a little that the Infant of Prague had most likely first been carved in Spain in the 1340s, but then it didn't surprise him too much. The Spanish fellas he'd stopped to play guitar with when he was on the beat in Brooklyn, they loved statues, and a lot of them shared his own feeling for wood. He remembered a guy named Rodriguez, over on Fourth Avenue, who had asked him to come into his apartment one day, just to show off his collection of Exact-O knives. Those were the days.

It surprised Pasquale a little more to find out that the original Infant held a bird, not a globe with a cross, in his right hand. All the religious birds he remembered belonged to Saint Francis. If a bird did come to the Infant, why didn't he land on his crown, the highest point, a natural perch? But the third Web site he saw said the Infant didn't get the crown until a procession in 1651. On the crown was inscribed this message: "He wishes to attract all hearts to His own through the attractiveness and simplicity of his Divine image." Of course this didn't explain why the Infant had acquired over the years at least 70, maybe as many as 85, different outfits, nine of which were kept in the Museum of the Infant of Prague.

When he clicked on the Museum's site, Pasquale noticed that they sold videos. One of the videos was a how-to video for dressing him. He would have the kids order it for Theresa. What the hell? They could order them all. Once they got here, he'd be out of the dog house and back on Easy Street.

An hour later, when Pasquale returned to the bedroom, Theresa was gone. He was about to go back downstairs, to make himself a peanut butter, *prosciutt'* and *muzzarell'* sandwich, when he spotted out of the corner of his eye two feet protruding from the gigantic closet he'd built when they'd moved in years ago. Since then, slowly but surely, his wife had managed to fill it with crap: dozens of pairs of shoes she never wore; a whole row of dresses that stopped fitting her after their second baby; on the floor metal boxes full of things he didn't even want to know about; and all the excess holiday decorations she couldn't fit in the attic or basement, both of which she'd also filled with crap. As he watched the little feet kick, he realized he had to face facts: His wife was a hoarder.

"Terry?"

He heard her muffled voice, watched the little toes curl as she tried to pull herself out. If he laughed, God would forgive him.

A few seconds later, he saw the head.

"Don't help me out," she said sarcastically.

"I didn't want to disturb you."

"Your sister's ass, Pattelli. What do you want?"

"I was doing a little research on the Infant of Prague."

Crawling on her hands and knees, Theresa grabbed their 200-pound, Kennedy-Era nightstand, and, grimacing, pulled herself to her feet. She turned to face her husband, who, in his old dress pants, fleece jacket and baseball cap, looked like she-didn't-know-what.

"What do you want, Pasquale, a medal?"

"You wanted to know about him."

Theresa walked past her husband as though he were a much less important statue than the one she hoped to find.

"*You* wanted to know about him, Pattelli," she said over her shoulder. "I just want to know where the hell he is."

"Is it so important, Theresa? I didn't even finish the *bresebria* yet. One of the Wise Men's arms is broken off, and I'm missing a sheep."

Theresa was out of patience.

"If it's not important to you, it doesn't matter. So why don't you call your holy-roller sister, and go see where you both gotta go."

Pasquale left the room dejected. Theresa exhaled, and lay back on the bed. Why did she really need to find this thing? When she and her husband were first married, the statue stood in a corner of their uncluttered bedroom, watching over them as they tried for six years, without success, to have a baby. Whenever they made love, she could see the eyes watching her, could catch a glimpse of the Infant's crown, and she'd remember part of the Little Crown rosary, "And the Word was made flesh." And she'd remember that the statue was in fact an infant and seemed to want to be the only infant in the room, the only object of her attention, even while she was satisfying Pasquale, who was still the only man she'd ever known in that way.

She knew now as she'd known then that the statue had power. Her great-aunt Giuseppina had given it to her, telling her it had been hand-painted in Rome. Is this what cardinals did in their spare time, painted statues of pretty babies that were supposed to be little Christs? To tell the truth, it bothered her now the way it did back then, but she couldn't just give it away. Only an Italian, maybe a Polack, could appreciate it. But all the Italians and Polacks she'd known in her new suburb already had one, usually handed down from their own great-aunts before they died somewhere in the Bronx or Brooklyn or Queens. And it would have been a sin to sell it. So at the end of the sixth childless year of her marriage, she took the Infant down from its marble and gold pedestal (also a gift from her aunt) and put it on the floor next to her dresser, in a spot she couldn't see from her side of the bed. Her husband still had a view of it from his side, but what difference did that make? When he was home, he missed half of what was right in front of his nose. Not that he would think too hard about it anyway while they were in bed. Like her mother used to say, a man's thing has no conscience.

Two months after she put the Infant in his new place, she was pregnant. She'd thought then this meant he was holy, watching over them until the time was right. Now maybe she thought it meant something different. Either way, she wanted him out now, for strength to deal with the Pope again, and to make sure her irresponsible son wouldn't get this blond girl — whose family *claimed* to be Italian — pregnant before he was sure the marriage was right.

†††
†

Evelyn and Peter sat at desks stationed at far corners of their L-shaped living room. Evelyn was surfing the Internet, trying to forget impending work, through online shopping.

"Sweetheart, take a look at this."

At moments like this one, Peter understood that married life would require a constant willingness to be interrupted. In theory the interruptions annoyed him, even when they came from someone as well intentioned as his fiancee. In practice they were a relief. For as much as he aspired to do good work, grade his students' papers promptly, write carefully, pay his bills punctually, answer his email conscientiously, Peter was, in his heart, like the lion, or maybe the hyena, who hunted with great energy in brief spurts, but preferred to spend most of his time lying in the grass, waiting for a willing female to distract him. He shut down his computer, yawned, and shuffled over to Evelyn's desk.

"What do you have?"

Her screen displayed an array of rings.

"What do you think of these? They're replicas."

"Of what?"

"Antique engagement rings."

Peter smiled, but his hands clenched, pressed down on the back of Evelyn's swivel chair.

"Babe, my neck. You know how I feel about you grabbing my chair."

Marriage would also require attention to detail. He ignored the complaint and studied the rings.

"I like them."

"I like this one."

Evelyn pointed the cursor arrow at a setting called "The Edwardian."

"It's an Edwardian-style ring with a crown basket and tulip-shaped v's covered with round bead-set diamonds on a pavè shank."

"Okay."

He hovered between boredom and horror at the sticker price, but could see Evelyn's disappointment with his lack of enthusiasm. As she rolled her tense shoulders, he realized he had to think fast. He kissed her on the cheek, buying himself a few seconds, keeping his lips on her until he felt confident in his way out. Then he straightened up and announced, "No matter what you pick, Honey, our wedding's gonna be great, wherever you decide we should have it: Florida, Italy, New York, Las Vegas, a church, a house, a field. Whatever you want . . . ten people, a hundred. Whatever happens, it'll be the happiest day of my life. You'll see."

Evelyn kept her eyes on the screen

"Uh-huh," she answered flatly. "See, I like this one here, because it reminds me of the engagement ring my cousin Luciano took from our grandmother when she died. I loved that ring, but he won't give it up. And it's not like he needs it."

"Look. If this is the ring you want, we'll get it."

Peter was learning the irrelevance of practicality in planning for a wedding.

"I love you," he announced, planting another kiss on the cheek, and walking back to his desk.

"And," he added, "for the record, I'm leaning toward elopement to Italy. Type in 'Italian wedding' and see what comes up."

Evelyn laughed.

"We should only be so lucky."

Young Marcello and the Pope sat on ebony chairs upholstered with gold velvet. Marcello had thought to have them carried here, to a balcony facing the gardens, to take full advantage of the warm January day. The Pope appeared to be enjoying the luxury of outdoor privacy and comfort. He sat serenely watching the Vatican landscapers work their magic.

"Your Grace, we received yesterday this letter from New York, in America."

"I have been there, Marcello. I know where it is. Please."

"It is as though it fell from the heavens."

"As though? Have you not yet learned to see the Divine Hand in all things?"

"Of course. . . ."

"Are you going to read it, or shall I have to do so myself, and in the process lose another precious portion of what little eyesight God has left me that I might discern the few beauties and many evils of this world?"

Marcello brandished the letter and began.

"Dear Holy Father,

I'm writing with a personal appeal. Please forgive me if I don't write as well as I should, but my family didn't send girls to Catholic school, so I had to take the secretarial track at New Utrecht.'"

The Pope raised a finger.

"Utrecht?"

"Yes, Your Grace."

"Are we not at odds with the Union of Utrecht?"

"Less so, Eminence, since Vatican Two, but this Utrecht is a high school in Brooklyn. Shall I continue?"

"Please, hurry. . . . Lately, I find my attention flagging. Perhaps it is the onset of dementia, which at this point, would arrive as a mercy."

Marcello read on.

"'My son wants to get married, but his future wife will only marry him if you perform the ceremony. Father, he's been living in sin, and this is the only way to get him out. You might remember him. He was almost Pope before you.'"

A flash of recognition illuminated the Pope's creviced face. At that moment Guglielmo appeared from the velvet curtain behind them, wheeling a media cart with dvd player and monitor. Marcello nodded, signaling Guglielmo to hit the play button. The black and white footage, the work of a security camera, pictures a stocky woman, clearly American in her voluble speech and accent. The woman is sitting in a Vatican office. She wears a flowing purple dress. Flanked by four men, two on either side of her, one of whom holds her hand, she faces a cardinal and his two attendants.

The Pope recognized the cardinal immediately as Belmonte, a local and one of the Vatican's enforcers. He arched an eyebrow.

A priest, by his vestments a monsignor, seated next to the large American woman, addresses Belmonte in Italian, explaining the potential appeal of the woman's son as the next Pope. Belmonte acknowledges the argument with a condescending wave of his hand, then speaks in a manner that both denigrates the woman and her claims, and angrily admits of their inevitability under the circumstances. The American woman grips the arms of her chair and begins shouting something in English. The cardinal is then seen to lower his head and actually push his chair and inch or two back from her as she speaks. Eventually, he folds his hands and nods, then, almost as if it pains him to do so, makes the sign of the cross over her. The video cuts to a crimson screen.

"This woman is the author of the letter," Marcello explained.

"I see."

"And it is true, as Your Holiness will recall, that under intense media scrutiny and pressure from the parliament at Montecitorio, the Vatican honored what she claimed to be sacred visions of both her son and husband, and consented to name the former, one Peter Pattelli, a layman, as the first American Pope. Of course consent came with the conditions that Cardinal Belmonte would in essence supervise his papacy, and the Vatican would reserve the right to limit his contact with her and other family members."

"Good Lord, is the woman Italian?"

Marcello nodded.

"You can understand now perhaps why she withdrew her young Peter as a candidate."

"Indeed."

"The Letter continues:

'So I'm asking that you save my son's soul, by marrying him to the girl he thinks he loves.'

Then she goes on to make a veiled threat about launching a global campaign to re-popularize the Infant of Prague."

"For what possible reason?"

"Perhaps to challenge Your Eminence's iconic hegemony, although she states it not in so many words."

"But this is truly providential, Marcello. The hand of God."

"And of Theresa Pattelli."

"If this saintly Theresa only knew how well her request would serve our purpose: spotlighting the Pope as supreme broker of earthly love. Ah, marvelous, I'll step up my workout regimen. Now, is the bride also one of our flock?"

"I believe she is."

"Pity, I could have converted her as an overture to the opera, but we mustn't expect gifts beyond those that the Lord lays in our laps."

"Your Grace, there is one bit of business to conduct in connection with her proposal. The letter goes on to say that by the time we read this, Theresa will have arrived in Rome, with the mother of the bride, to request a face-to-face meeting."

"Is this necessary?"

Marcello whistled and looked out over the gardens.

"Wouldn't word of our consent suffice?"

His eyes narrowing, Marcello answered, "You've seen the video, Your Grace."

† †
†

Theresa and Rose Ann ran their hands up and down the arms of their red velvet-upholstered chairs. Rose Ann patted one arm with an open palm.

"My Nanna Annalise had chairs just like this in her front parlor."

"They're beautiful," said Theresa. "I hope you didn't throw them out."

Rose Ann flinched as though she'd been hit in the arm by a rock.

"Oh, no. Why would I do something like that?"

"Some people don't appreciate beautiful things."

"Hmmm. I know just what you mean, Theresa. These kids today don't understand what it was to have no furniture at all. When my daddy had to give up his business, we lived for three years without a couch or a dining room table. We were lucky we had a bed."

"My brother Dominick slept on the floor, but we were happy."

"Isn't that the truth?"

At that very moment the women heard a knock at the ten foot-high door. Marcello entered.

"Ah, Signora Pattelli e Signora Cavaluzzo. Buon giorno."

Marcello shook the women's hands as though cradling baby birds.

"It is truly *un piacere*, a pleasure. . . . Please, please, take a seat. As they say in America, make yourselves comfortable. His Eminence will arrive momentarily. He looks forward to making your acquaintance."

Theresa and Rose Ann sat down again. Marcello moved another, less grand chair close to theirs. As he dusted the seat, Theresa spoke.

"I've seen him on television. He looks very nice . . . the Pope."

Marcello hesitated.

"Yes, indeed. The Pope is — How would you say this? — a Pope for the people. For you."

Rose Ann smoothed her bangs.

"He does have a way about him."

Another knock on the door lifted Marcello from his chair. He crossed the room, and opened the door, to reveal the pontiff in full white and gold regalia, erect as a tin soldier. He entered slowly, head bowed. Rose Ann practically leapt to her feet, and turned around to pull Theresa almost as quickly up. As the Pope approached them, he raised his head, meeting the women's eyes with a penetrating gaze and knit brows, feeling he was achieving the proper effect. He made the largest Sign of the Cross Theresa had ever seen, and signaled to his attendants in the doorway, who, immediately and with visible effort, wheeled in a fifteen foot-high gold throne mounted on a black marble base. The Pope took his place. He called Marcello over, to smooth folds of his robe which had gathered around his waist, then shifted with a grimace, and waved his attendant away.

Theresa attempted a slight curtsey.

"Theresa Pattelli, Your Highness."

Rose Ann crossed herself.

"Rose Ann Cavaluzzo, Father. God bless you."

The Pope gestured for them to sit down, remaining silent. What was the use of such interviews if one should fail to dignify the moment correctly? He allowed another pregnant few seconds to pass before finally acceding to practical matters.

"Please," he said, with a flourish of his right hand that invited the women to speak.

Rose Ann's jaw hung open. She unconsciously reached over to lay a hand on Theresa's arm. Theresa herself was enjoying the scene, but could feel an attack of sciatica coming on. It was time to get down to business.

"We're here, Your Honor, to ask a favor for our children."

The Pope sensed an opportunity for feigned naiveté and graceful condescension.

"We love to do what we can to help young people. I have been told little, so if you would be so kind, please explain what it is your children would like to request."

Theresa leaned forward.

"They won't ask anything themselves. Since what happened to him here a few years ago, my son acts like religion is a joke. Not that he didn't act that way before."

The Pope squirmed as imperceptibly as he could. This woman presented challenges he thought he had left behind in the pre-Vatican days. And his undergarments were binding him below.

Theresa continued.

"He laughs that we have your picture on the refrigerator. But I think," she said, watching Rose Ann for signs of alarm, "that he needs to come back to his senses. I try to tell him you don't have to believe everything you hear in the church to be a Catholic, but he's stubborn. Here he has her daughter, a beautiful girl."

Rose Ann beamed and squeezed Theresa's hand, happy she could set back and let this little powerhouse do the talking.

"He's got a beautiful girl who loves him, and he's living with her in sin."

Rose Ann's hand went limp.

"And they're no spring chickens, the two of them."

The Pope took a deep breath.

"I'm sorry if we're boring you, Father."

"No, no, my dear, I am simply not so young as I once was."

"We're all gettin' there. Anyway, that's why I have to ask you to marry them. Because otherwise we'll never see it."

Theresa saw the disturbance in Rose Ann's eyes, and realized she shouldn't play so fast and loose, even with a Pope whose personal history wasn't exactly a string of miracles. She knew what he wanted to hear.

"Besides, we think it's what God wants, for everyone to be married — in the church."

The Pope was relieved that his guests had reached the point of the request.

"Of course, I would be pleased to bring together two lovely young people before . . . Marcello, where could we expect to hold such a ceremony?"

Marcello appeared from the shadows.

"I would think, Your Grace, before the Great Basilica itself."

"Yes, it would be a lovely precedent, to perform the holy sacrament of matrimony before a throng of worshippers and Bernini's one hundred and some saints. Normally we deal only in blessings, but ah . . ."

The Pope clasped his hands together, and thought of himself in the third person.

". . . what a wonderful idea to have the Pope unite in matrimony a beautiful young woman and a young man who might himself have occupied this very seat, were it not for an unfortunate turn of events."

Theresa bit her lip.

"Yes," she said slowly, "they were very unfortunate."

"But, please," the Pope continued, "let us pray and say that we shall indeed transcend the events of the past, to establish a better kingdom here on earth, one more reflective of Christ's teachings and of the mission of his Holy Church. Let me offer then an official blessing of the union of your children. *In nomine Patris, et Figlii, et Spiritus Sancti.*"

As the Pope began, Rose Ann closed her eyes and saw in the darkness behind her lids an image of her oldest daughter, her pride and joy, gorgeous in her white silk dress, her wonderful man — the only one of Evelyn's beaus, to tell the truth, who had been the least bit respectful of her family — standing next to her. A beautiful blue light literally glowed from his eyes, as Peter lifted Evelyn's veil. The Pope, his scarlet cape opened like wings over a long white robe, floated over them, waving his hands in more benedictions than you could shake a hickory stick at. She'd waited all her life, two daughers, eighty years between 'em, and this was her first chance at the wedding she'd always dreamt of, the one she could never quite have for herself. The joy was almost too much, and then she heard Theresa's voice.

"Excuse me, Father, but while you're at it, can we add one more prayer, for good weather?"

Marcello looked up at the pontiff, amazed.

The Pope cleared his throat, and without raising his head answered, "It is unusual to interrupt a papal blessing."

Rose Ann swallowed hard and opened one eye to peek at the action. Theresa again.

"I don't know if you've ever been to Florida, Your Holiness, but the one time I was there, to visit my sister-in-law's mother in her condominium — which I told my husband we should have bought when she died — the weather was stifling. Then on the way home, we flew through a monsoon. So maybe if you could just ask God for a nice breeze."

"But," Marcello interjected, "what does this have to do with a wedding in Vatican City?"

Theresa looked directly at the Pope, who still refused to open his eyes.

"That's what I wanted to say before you all started making plans. The wedding has to be in Florida."

Rose Ann found the courage to speak, furrowing her brow, her voice lamentation itself.

"I have so much family, Father, and they're so old. They just can't travel."

"That's right," Theresa added. "It's not like my husband and I love to fly. I find the seats very uncomfortable. But it's only fair. She's paying the bill."

The Pope opened his eyes.

"Florida?"

"It is in the southern United States, Your Grace."

"Yes, Marcello," the Pope said wearily, then under his breath in the page's direction, "you will recall that the Vatican museum includes a hall of maps."

The Pope turned to the women.

"Gentle women, could we not persuade you to permit us the honor of hosting the glorious conjugation of your progeny?"

"Well, I don't know," Rose Ann began, half-whispering, before Theresa jumped in.

"If that means you still want to do it here, the answer's no."

Theresa pulled a handful of photos from her purse.

"Please, Father, take a look a these."

She got up and walked over to the Pope's throne.

"This," she said pointing, "is a picture of my husband outside his shop. The things next to him are eight-foot-high wooden scale models of Florida and New York State. They're for the reception. What good would they be here? Do you know how long it would take him to do Italy?"

She laid other the pictures in the Pope's lap.

"And I think you'll find these very interesting."

He studied them for a moment.

"What are they?"

"What? You don't recognize them?"

"Is this one a likeness of me?"

Theresa chuckled.

"I think Your Worship needs a new eyeglass prescription. No, this is insurance, in case you're not willing to come to Tampa. This is the world's largest Infant of Prague. My husband carved it from a solid block of poplar wood. My daughter's artist boyfriend — He's a dreamer — did the painting. I made the suit. Now, look at this next one. This is the Infant's pet dog, the Puppy of Prague. He's cute. People would love him. And this picture is the Infantmobile. My husband modified a golf cart. If you say no, then our kids won't get married, and we'll have a lot of time on our hands to take the Infantmobile on a world tour. The Chinese'll go crazy. But if you cooperate, we'll just put the Infant at the back of the catering hall. And then this one is you with Father Maciel, the Mexican. You know, the one who started Regnum Dei."

With a mixture of wonder and confusion playing on her face like an atonal symphony, Rose Ann studied Theresa, who kept pressing the pontiff, who himself, Rose Ann noticed, was suddenly as pale as sand.

"The Legion of Christ. If I remember right, they locked up nuns, didn't they? Your own visitation said so. And then there were the boys. Maybe we need to remind people."

Theresa lifted the photos from the Pope's lap, put them in her purse, walked back to her chair, and sat down, triumphant. The Pope cast a pleading glance to Marcello, as if to say, "It would be easier to distribute money to every Catholic across the globe." Then, with his right hand, he made a grand gesture of resignation.

"So be it. We shall draw the eyes of the Catholic world to Florida."

He smiled sheepishly at Theresa and Rose Ann.

"And of course in the process perform a joyous sacrament for two young people who may at least bear children representing the future of God's Holy Church."

Theresa reached over and held Rose Ann's hand.

"We should all be so lucky."

† †

†

"You're lucky we were even able to get the Pope," Theresa told her son. "Without him, how would you marry the mush-mush?"

"Who?"

"Your girlfriend. Your fiancee."

"But do we really have to do Pre-Cana? What is Pre-Cana anyway?"

"You should know that. All your cousins went through it. The priest talks to you about marriage."

"What do priests know about marriage?"

"Don't be smart. They see a lot of people get married. Father Yablonski married half the people in our parish. And the monsignor knows most of the couples who come to Mass by their first names. He could tell you stories."

Peter took another sip of his mother's weak coffee. On this chilly a day, he would drink straight hot water. But why couldn't she add to her percolator another couple of tablespoons of whatever canned coffee she'd gotten on sale this week? She was Italian. Even his WASPiest girlfriends had known better. Maybe if he just stopped complaining about it and looked unhappy, she'd change the proportions.

"So that's it? We just talk to the priest?"

"Not exactly. You need to meet a certain number of hours with a married couple. Your counselors."

"I don't want to talk to other people about my marriage before it even happens."

"You don't talk. You listen."

"You don't say."

"They tell you what to expect. And they ask you questions."

"What kind of questions?"

"I'll let you know."

"What do you mean?"

"Since I knew you wouldn't want to talk to strangers, I cut a deal with the Pope. Your father and I are gonna be your counselors."

Pasquale had studied. He wanted to know his stuff. Go by the book, like he did on the force. But there were a few books. They called them "Pre-Cana inventories." You had the New Horizons, for the remarried, which, thank the Good Lord, his son didn't need. Then you had FOCCUS (Facilitating Open Couple Communication, Understanding & Study), which was a little too liberal for his taste, but which his wife thought was more realistic. Then, finally, the one he featured, PREPARE/ENRICH, which also stood for something, and stuck more to the old rules.

His son was a little weird, but he was basically a good boy, and this *biondina* he was marrying was a good girl. She talked like a lady, and she had even asked Pasquale if she could come along to church one Sunday this month. Maybe with the right Pre-Cana and a weekly after-church custard, Peter would go back too — for good. Sure, some Sundays Pasquale himself was tired, and instead of actually going to the church he watched the Mass in Latin on the Catholic channel. But on those days the boy could come over and watch with him. Then for lunch they could have a nice bowl of macaronis *aglia-ul'* with fennel sausage. Something light.

And if the kids weren't too old — Peter had to be at least forty, and the girl had a few miles on her too, but his own mother had given birth to her last child at forty-six, so it was in God's hands — maybe they'd give him and Theresa a grandchild. That would be nice. If it was a girl, he could build her a dollhouse; if it was a boy, he could teach him how to use the router. But it would be safety first. He'd buy a little pair of goggles for his grandson to wear around the shop. And Theresa would be happy, so she'd cook more. These days she'd been tending toward rigatoni, which, he didn't want anyone to get him wrong, weren't bad, but weren't as good as the linguini and angel hair she used to make when Peter and Delores were small. Especially with the white clam sauce. A grandchild could bring it back.

But where was his wife? They were supposed to be at the bed and breakfast by four-thirty. They were going the weekend retreat route. Further out on Long Island. Theresa had booked adjoining rooms. He sat down at the piano. Chopin was good for calming the nerves, but when you wanted to hurry your wife up, you went with Verdi. Something from *Trovatore*. He pulled out the sheet music for "Stride La Vampa!" and started to play the opening. Then footsteps above.

"I'm coming, Pasquale. The toilet wouldn't flush."

His fingers still tapping the keys, he answered, "Too much paper, Terry."

He was happy now, and ready to find out how much about Pre-Cana he would really have to remember. The kids were studious, so he'd have to seem at least to be on top of things. He was pretty sure he could handle "Self-Awareness" and "Morality in Marriage," but he hoped his wife was up for topics like "Liturgical Planning" and "Intimacy and Sexuality." God forbid he should have to remember all the steps of the Billings Ovulation Method. He'd throw one question at Theresa, just to see where he stood. If he could, he'd play *faccia dost'*. She appeared on the staircase.

"Terry, why do they call it 'Pre-Cana' again?"

Theresa spoke first.

"It's like turning water into wine."

"What is, Mom?"

"The Pre-Cana."

His mother's smile told Peter she had swallowed a scriptural canary.

Curling her lip ever so slightly, Theresa spoke as though Peter weren't there, to Evelyn, who sat on the edge of the guest room bed, holding Peter's hand.

"I'll bet my son didn't know it comes from the water-into-wine miracle."

Theresa studied her son's, her future daughter-in-law's and finally her husband's eyes for a flash of recognition that never came.

"What are you talking about, Terry? Give us a hint."

"The wedding feast at Cana."

"Oh, Cana," Pasquale repeated, looking to his son, who shrugged his shoulders, for help. "That's, ah . . ."

"It's in Galilee, Pattelli. On the Sea of Galilee. For your information, that's where's Christ got four of the apostles."

She turned to Peter and Evelyn.

"You might want to know that, if you're getting married by the Pope."

Pasquale piped up.

"Oh, the fishing there must be very nice. But I thought Christ was a carpenter, not a fisherman. What was he doing by the sea?"

"It's not a real sea, Pasquale. It's a lake. Four of the apostles fished there. You go to Mass every week. Are you too busy bs-ing to listen to the readings? Anyway, it was very popular with the Jews, like Miami Beach. Christ went there to preach to them."

Evelyn fidgeted and began twirling a lock of her hair.

"Mom, I hate to interrupt, but what are we actually supposed to talk about here?"

Theresa pulled out a single sheet of paper from the leather portfolio in her lap, and pulled her chair closer to the bed.

"This is our agenda."

She glanced over at Pasquale, who remained in his chair by the window overlooking Peconic Bay. He was less trouble over there, so she left him alone. She continued, her voice achieving a quasi-official tone.

"You may have noticed that your father and I are very compatible."

Peter squeezed Evelyn's hand and bit his lip. Theresa looked again at Pasquale — at that moment cleaning the inside of his ear with a handkerchief — sighed, and returned her gaze to the betrothed.

"I'm not saying he's easy to live with, but we understand each other. Do you two understand each other?"

Peter barely understood himself most days, but on this day, as Evelyn's fingers interlaced with his; and as she listened dutifully and cleared her throat; and as he thought about how through this politeness sometimes emerged — usually thanks to his suggesting she wasn't handling work pressure well or was inviting a friend from out of town to sleep on their couch at an inopportune time — a ferocity of purpose and conviction of moral rectitude that he not only loved but admired. He knew that, even though his mother wasn't Evelyn's flesh and blood, and even though Evelyn only reluctantly spoke about her emotional life to anyone but him, his future wife would carry the burden, and give the illustrious Mrs. Pattelli an answer that would move things along. Knowing this was enough for him to begin.

"Mom, let me say this . . ."

Theresa cut in.

"Because if you don't understand each other, you shouldn't get married, especially since you've been out of the church so long."

"Mom, technically we've never been out."

"Who's kidding who, Peter Boy? When was your last confession? Which, by the way, you have to give before you get married. So we can turn water into wine."

"What?"

"Like the miracle. It's a metaphor."

She spoke to Evelyn.

"A writer like my son should know what that means."

Suddenly they heard Pasquale's voice.

"It's like the Pope. He's not really God on earth, but we say he is. So people see the church as holy. That's how we keep up appearances. The glue of society, kids."

"That's right," Theresa continued. "We want everyone to see the two of you like wine, not water. When you live in sin, in the city, with your friends who act like irresponsible *cidruls'*, you're water."

Theresa spoke to Peter.

"Your fiancee's mother and I want you to be wine. Look at her husband.

He wouldn't get married in the church. Then he took off with a barmaid."

Peter couldn't help himself.

"Now that's a mixed metaphor."

Evelyn came to life.

"My parents were married for nine years."

Theresa caught sight of her husband heading for the door.

"Where are you going, Pasquale?"

"Breakfast started a half-hour ago, Theresa. I'd thought I'd get a corn muffin, and come back."

"We'll go later. Together."

Pasquale sat back down, arms crossed, like a child in time out.

Theresa spoke again to Evelyn.

"It doesn't matter. For your father it was easy go, easy come."

Peter laughed.

"Go ahead, make fun of me. I can't help it that I didn't get to go to college and daydream for four years."

She pulled another sheet of paper from her portfolio.

"Just remember, everything's funny until you're paying alimony. Anyway, I'm supposed to read you this. Listen. Here: 'The Church rejoices with you as you prepare for marriage. Allow me to personally assure you of my care and concern for you in the weeks and months ahead. You may have been very close to the Church throughout your lives, and you now look forward to the assistance that the Church will provide in preparing you for marriage. Or you may be returning to the Church after a period of being away. Welcome home.'"

Pasquale walked to the bed and pulled Peter and Evelyn close to him for a bear hug.

"Welcome home, kids."

"O. K., Pattelli. They get the idea."

Pasquale returned to his seat, to watch the baymen come in with their morning's catch.

"So, do you understand each other?" Theresa asked.

Peter and Evelyn nodded.

"Good. Then we can move to Item Two: your expectations. What do you expect out of marriage?"

Evelyn seized the moment.

"I expect my husband to be faithful to me, in all ways."

Theresa stared at her only son.

"Of course you do. You're Sicilian. But good luck with that one."

Peter bristled.

"What's that supposed to mean?"

Theresa immediately turned her gaze to Evelyn.

"Nothing. It's just that my son isn't like his friend Ryan. Ryan was a drinker, but once he got serious about a girl, he settled down and married her, and now they have kids. My son likes to get serious. He moves right in. Then he loves 'em and leaves 'em."

Peter began to suspect this line of questioning was more a meticulously planned tribulation than part of any rote test. This was his mother's tough love, which he decided — a instinctive decision that surprised even him — to meet with gentle play, allowing a sense of absurd communion to replace the anger welling in his heart.

"So you're saying with me it's easy go, easy come?"

"Don't be smart," Theresa answered. "As a matter of fact, I did the math."

"What math?"

"The math of your life."

"Oh, Son, your mother was always top of her class in math."

"It's not difficult math, Pasquale. If you take all our son's serious relationships with girls from the time he left the house until Evelyn — according to my list, that's Anne Marie, Bridget, Ellie and Samantha — you see that he averages about two years and two months per."

Evelyn shot Peter a sad look that left him no choice but to defend himself.

"What? I was in my twenties and thirties. I bet that's pretty good compared to the national average."

Theresa kept a hard face.

"I hope you don't think you're in this for just two years. This is the Pope we're talking about. And then we have to get everybody down to Florida. And I know things are cheaper there, but I bet Rose Ann is spending a pretty penny."

Evelyn sensed a chance to deflect the assault.

"I can give you the numbers."

"See, Peter. Your fiancee knows. Nothing's cheap. And even when the cow's expensive, that doesn't mean the milk won't be sour sometimes. Of course Evelyn's no cow. God knows, you could afford to eat more, dear. And then there's the honeymoon. Key West is very nice, but you're father and I went there on a cruise, the Eastern Caribbean cruise, and we spent a month's heating bill in one day."

"Remember the grouper sandwiches, Terry. Oh, kids, they melted in your mouth."

"So make sure you have the right expectations, so you can stay together. And start with the honeymoon."

Theresa finally smiled at her husband, who took it as a signal to turn his chair toward the action.

"Your father took me to Bermuda, which we paid for ourselves, since his father never worked and my father spent all his money on schemes."

Surveying the room — faux-Victorian upholstered chair, stick-on bordering on the walls, rayon bed cover and shag carpeting — Theresa reminisced.

"Our room was much nicer than this one. We had a balcony and a view of the Atlantic. We could watch the colored waiters bring drinks out to the beach. And the beaches were pink."

"Sounds like a colonial watercolor," Peter remarked.

"We met some very nice colored fellas there, Son."

Theresa rode along on the vapor trail of memory.

"They were very nice, but I couldn't understand their accents."

"There's a lot of history in Bermuda. After you're married, we can all go back, and your mother and I can stay in the same hotel."

Pasquale was positively doe-eyed.

"I took your mother skeet shooting there. She even water skied."

"I thought the first night at the hotel would be the most romantic night of my life. But my husband drank so many Mai Tais at dinner that he got sick and couldn't. . . ."

"Ah, Terry, I still think it was the sauce they put on the veal."

"Whatever, Pattelli, the point is we spent the first night of our romantic life together with your head over a toilet bowl."

She turned to Peter.

"Try not to do things like that to your wife-to-be."

"Sure, Mom. Can we go on to what's next?"

"O. K. Family background."

Peter feared the worst, and put his arm around Evelyn's shoulders.

"Tell me about your childhood."

"Wait," Peter said. "That's not fair. The only childhood you don't know about is Evelyn's."

"And maybe you don't know everything either."

Evelyn crinkled her brow. Her future mother-in-law was methodical.

"Your father left when you were nine. How did that make you feel?"

Evelyn slumped down and began twirling her hair again.

"It made me feel terrible. Of course. I was depressed. I had a mom and dad, a beautiful house on the water, ballet lessons, and a month later I was living in a dangerous neighborhood with my grieving mother, who was angry all the time."

"Is she still angry? Is that why you took so long to get married?"

"Hold on, Mom."

"What? Who would want to get married after that?"

"I don't think I saw it that way. The rest of my family had a lot of good marriages."

"So you say."

Evelyn began to shake. If they just got up and left now, Peter thought, he might be able to talk Evelyn into Las Vegas.

"Mom, this isn't supposed to be an inquisition, is it?"

"Sarah Bernhardt: You're very dramatic. I'm not the Gestapo."

Pasquale leapt at the chance to comment on World War II.

"They were bastards, Son. Don't let anybody kid you."

Evelyn didn't make a move to leave, so Peter knew he would have to put his foot down.

"O. K. Let's move on. What's left?"

"Intimacy and sexuality."

Evelyn and Peter exclaimed together, "Oh, God."

When he heard the last word out of his wife's mouth, Pasquale shifted his eyes and mind towards the bay. Thin clouds were drifting in from the west: a good sign. The tide was high and still coming in. It was a little cool for early April, but all right. On a day like today you didn't have to worry about mosquitos. Two men in waders and heavy vests were standing in shin-deep water, surfcasting. He guessed they were going for flounder. They could be using squid or sandworms. Or better yet, clam bellies.

Peter prayed that his mother wouldn't ask the kind of general but direct question he was all but certain she would.

"How's your intimate life?"

Evelyn hung in.

"If you mean our emotional life, I think we're very close and honest with each other. When I sense something's bothering Peter, I always ask how he's doing or what's the matter. And he does the same with me. I think our communication is very good."

At that moment Peter was happy he had chosen an Italian woman seemingly as determined and decisive as his mother.

"What about sex?"

Peter leapt in.

"We have it."

"How often?"

"Mom, this is why Pre-Cana should be left to strangers."

"What do you know about Pre-Cana? Just answer the question."

"Enough."

"I'm very satisfied with our intimate life," Evelyn concluded.

"What about my son? You never know with him."

To Peter.

"Who was the girl who wouldn't sleep with you?"

"Amanda. Why do you know that?"

"Your sister talks."

"Wonder where she gets it from."

"This isn't about me. It's about the two of you."

"Really?"

"Of course. Now, this Amanda: You stayed with her even though you weren't happy."

"I loved her."

Evelyn dropped her head a tiny bit.

"How can you say that in front of your wife?"

"I'm sure Evelyn loved other boyfriends too. And she had problems with them. And she stayed with them for years, in spite of the problems."

Theresa clicked her pen and made a note.

"I'll get to that. But why did you stay with a woman who wouldn't have sex with you?"

"Look, now and then she would, and, as you pointed out, I only stayed with her for about two point two years."

Peter looked to his father observing the fishermen. He seemed so peaceful. Pasquale turned and met his son's eye. He mouthed the word "squid."

"And besides, you were with Dad for four years before you got married. And according to you, in those days respectable women didn't have sex before marriage."

"I didn't. Some women did, like my sister-in-law. Once she opened her legs, your Uncle Paul didn't stand a chance."

The comparison with his dead brother's wife drew Pasquale back in.

"Son, even my mother said your mother was the best of them all."

Theresa embellished.

"We waited, because we both wanted to wait. Your father was a gentleman."

"Plus," Pasquale added, rising from his chair, and thinking now that they really ought to wrap this up before the breakfast buffet was totally wiped out, "we could always find ways to bend the rules."

††
 †

On Sunday, May 3rd, the Infant of Prague's feast day, the Pope, his attendants, and a tempermental Vatican camera crew entered the Church of

Our Lady of Perfect Holiness, in the Ybor City section of Tampa. Ybor had once been a thriving community of "Latins," the local name for the hodge-podge of Italian, Spanish and Cuban Americans who staffed the local cigar factories and populated the eponymous shacks that filled the neighborhood. The Latins had long since fled for sparser sections of Tampa or its suburbs, giving way first to African Americans, then to the local Bohemian crowd, and finally to a few young professionals and many tourists. Rose Ann, like many of the Ybor refugees, still drove the half-hour across town, to attend social events at the now-landmark Italian Club or Sunday Mass at O. L. P. H. In their younger days, these refuguees made sure their children, like Evelyn, went to Catholic school there, even if these same children would years later return, like Evelyn, as hipsters who sought refuge from bubble-headed beach culture, at Goth nightspots like The Castle.

When the Pope and his entourage entered the church grounds, his face registered satisfaction. It was a warm but not hot day. The myrtle trees were just coming into bloom. And of course the gardenias were bursting forth, perfuming his entry and reminding him, as he spied the hideous new condominiums across the parking lot and adjacent to the *autostrada* or highway or whatever the Americans liked to call it, that the Holy Church could still provide an oasis for harried souls. The thought sweetened his mission here. He looked forward now to the nuptials, assuming afterward that good Cuban food would abound.

Marcello returned the Pope's smile, as he directed the camera crew to take their places near the front entrance of the church. Several minutes later the first limousine rolled up. Rose Ann Cavaluzzo emerged. She scanned the church grounds until she spotted the Pope around the side of the church, where he stood sniffing a red flower. It would be terrible to interrupt him, but as mother of the bride — and God knows in this case that was no small chore — she felt like she had the right.

"Hello, Your Grace. Do you like our grounds?"

"Ah, Signora Cavaluzzo. It is a strange thing. I always thought these . . . How are they called?"

"Hibiscus. My favorite. We had a shrub in front of my house before the beetles got it."

"Yes, the hibiscus. It was my impression that they had a fragrance."

Rose Ann felt as though she should apologize for the staple Florida plant. "Well, I . . ."

The Pope waved off her budding explanation.

"I understand. Some things are more beautiful from afar."

As a Catholic, could she take offense at something the Pope said?

Guglielmo and one of the cameramen approached. The younger page spun his index finger in a circle, to indicate that the camera was rolling. Immediately, the Pope laid hands on Rose Ann's shoulders.

"My good woman, you must be extremely proud of your parish's devotion, expressed through such an exquisite garden."

Noticing the camera, Rose Ann fluffed her teased hair and smiled broadly.

"Well, we are proud. And proud of our girl too. She's gonna make a great bride."

"Of this, we have no doubt," replied the Pope on cue. "Now, shall we step inside the church?

"Ah, before we do, Your Holiness, I was hoping I could ask just a single favor."

Guglielmo made a slit-throat gesture, for the cameraman to cut.

"I was hoping that you might not mind adding a little something to the blessing."

The Pope scowled and stared at Guglielmo, who shrugged his shoulders.

On her home turf now, Rose Ann was undaunted. She removed from her white handbag a large, laminated index card.

"Just a little something about how important my family is to this community. Here. I wrote it out. Just a couple of sentences, really. The first part's about my daddy."

Conquering for the moment his annoyance, the Pope accepted the index card, and feigned interest.

"Was your father a member of this parish?"

"Well, not quite. But people in this town loved him. He did a lot of favors, just like you."

"Yes, I suppose in that case I could say a few words in his memory, and in the memory of . . ."

The pontiff strained his eyes to read the card. He spoke slowly.

"Uncle Charro?"

"My mother's brother. Now that man had class."

"Yes, I imagine."

"So just those two and maybe the other sentence about my *Nanna* Annalise. She was a saint in her own funny way."

The Pope raised his eyebrows.

"I don't mean to blaspheme, Father. I just . . ."

Again the Pope waved his hand in absolution, and sent Rose Ann along with a quick blessing. After which, he grabbed Guglielmo by the robe.

"But is it possible to keep this woman at bay?"

"I'm sure Marcello will have a solution."

"Remember, my son, if I am to involve myself personally in the sacrament of matrimony and thus electrify the Catholic world, we must find ways to keep the common people at the distance of, at the very least, an arm."

† †
†

At her mother's house, which had also been her grandmother's and great-grandmother's house (built by her great-grandfather), in the bedroom that was hers as a child, Evelyn sat at the edge of the bed, as two cousins pinned her hair and made up her face. In her hands she held a photo of her third grade O. L. P. H class, which included Randy Martinez, the boy who, in spite of his chubbiness and hyperhydrosis, was her first crush; and her best friend to this day, Angela Guzmán, who, half-German by birth and evangelical conservative by choice, now insisted that everyone super-Americanize her name by pronouncing it "GOOSE-man." Angela had been married for ten years, had three children, and was eternal sunshine itself. Evelyn loved her but knew she would harbor jealousy about Evelyn's being married by the Pope, even if her church saw him as an usurper of divine power. Then Evelyn imagined Angela as a white goose in a pink bridesmaid's dress, which made her chuckle.

"What's so funny, Ev?" her cousin Madeleine, an unmarried, big-boned good-ol' gal, asked.

Evelyn knew that Madeleine knew Angela well, and that in keeping with Italian Cousin Code, anything she said about Angela to Madeleine would get back to her best friend within a week.

"Nothing. I was just thinking about school at O. L. P. H."

"Thank God they knocked that school down, else my nephew would've had to go."

"You remember the nuns there?"

"Oh, those nuns. They were mean as snakes."

Evelyn nodded.

"Uh-huh. I remember the time they made me kneel on dried peas as a punishment."

"They did that to you?"

The sun through the window felt suddenly to Evelyn like it was burning her neck.

"It was a sunny day just like today. I remember Sister Margaret Rose took me out in front of the church, and sprinkled the dried peas right there on the sidewalk, with people walking by and everything."

"And now you're getting married there."

"That's funny, right? But, you know, I wouldn't want to get married anywhere else."

"Just to show her."

"Maybe. And just because I remember going to Mass there with *Nanna*."

"She'd be happy. Especially because you're having the reception at the Italian Club. Her mother and father donated a lot of time and money to build that thing."

A few times Evelyn had been with her family to the club, but it was the childhood Sunday afternoons with them she remembered best. All of them would be there at Nanna Annalise's kitchen table, worrying aloud over her not eating more, talking about how pretty and smart she was, and how well-behaved. She imagined them all in the back of the church, quiet as mice, smiling, and a little afraid of the Pope.

† †
†

The second limousine to arrive bore Theresa, Pasquale and Peter's sister Delores. Rose Ann was waiting by the curb to greet them.

"Why, Theresa, don't you look lovely."

"My daughter says purple's my color."

"Well, I have to agree. And how are you, sweetheart?"

"Oh, I feel terrific," Pasquale answered.

"Not you, Pattelli."

Delores didn't miss a beat.

"I feel good, too."

Now that the groom's family had arrived, Rose Ann felt free to worry about people she knew better. She stepped off the curb and looked quickly up and down the street.

"I hope my family's not gonna take too long. I swear, some of the them must've shown up late for their own birth."

Theresa walked up next to her.

"My son's the same way. He gets it from his father."

From her purple handbag Theresa pulled two hard candies, offering one to Rose Ann. The two mothers stood together, their mouths mildly puckered.

"We'll be lucky if he shows up at all."

Rose Ann's stomach knotted.

"Oh, no, you don't think he'll skip out?"

"No, it was just a figure of speech. He knows better."

Rose Ann took a deep breath and ushered Theresa to the sidewalk. The two took in the tall brick church, the white Madonna statue in front of the castellated rectory, and, again, the lush grounds.

"Very nice," Theresa said. "Where's the Pope?"

"I think he's in back. They told me he's resting."

"Who told you?"

"The camera crew."

Impressed, Theresa jutted out her lower lip.

"He should rest. He's not getting any younger."

"None of us are."

As they spoke, first one limousine, then another and another turned the corner and pulled in front of the church.

Rose Ann rushed again to the curb, calling to Theresa as she did.

"Now, this'll be my family."

Doors began to open. Watching from a distance, Theresa decided that all the women in this family would be skinny and energetic, but that she wouldn't hold it against them. And where was Pasquale? She spotted him standing on the church steps, with his head in the clouds.

"Come here, Pasquale."

"Look at this, Terry," he answered. "The stonemason did a very nice job with this insignia over the door. The two men on either side are rolling banana leaves."

Theresa shot a quick glance at the bas relief.

"Those are tobacco leaves, Pattelli. They made cigars here, like the ones Rose Ann bought you for Christmas?"

"Very interesting. I wonder if they used regular chisels."

"We can ask later. Now let's go. Here's the family."

Pasquale joined his wife on the sidewalk, and watched as a stream of good-looking women emerged from the cars. They looked like his own aunts, but with better bodies than he remembered his aunts ever having. It must have been the heat that kept them in shape. You burned off a lot of food down here. Even the older ones looked good. Very spry for their ages. And then came the men. They were thin too, but they moved more slowly. He'd heard from the kids about the grandfather's connections. Now he wondered if he recognized any of these faces from an organized crime chart. Pasquale kept watching, as Rose Ann made her way over.

"This is my family."

Theresa was getting overheated now, and tired of watching her husband watch other women.

"We guessed," she snapped.

"A very nice family," Pasquale added.

"I was hoping," Rose Ann explained, "to get them seated quick, before

Evelyn gets here. She has her own ideas about who oughtta sit where."

Theresa sympathized.

"They always have their own ideas."

Delores, listening in, rolled her eyes.

Rose Ann went on.

"And we have a little problem. Evelyn's father called me this morning. He's in town, and he wants to help give her away, which is something I promised to her Uncle Nunzio, who really deserves to do it."

Delores could see from the expression on her mother's face that she was secretly pleased with the unfolding drama, which, honestly, she herself was happy to encourage. Anything to make this all a little less boring. It wouldn't be as good as her brother marrying into an Irish family, but still. The spark needed just a little air to start a fire. She locked arms with her father and led him to the garden, where she could slip him a cigarette he wasn't supposed to have and they could smoke in peace. They'd come back when things got a little more intense.

By the time he reached the church, Peter was already exhausted from a week of drinking and socializing with in-laws. But even though his head ached, he wore a calcified smile as he slid from the limousine, whose New Yorker of a driver had, for nearly an hour, regaled him and his New Yorker groomsmen with tales of how "extra-smokin'" Florida girls were in bed. Judging from the number of limos and cars in the church lot, most of the audience for the wedding were inside by now. In a couple of hours Peter would be eating crab empanada and mini-meatball hors d'oeuvres, and sipping a frozen daquiri next to his beautiful new wife, just hours from their wedding night in the most expensive hotel on Indian Rocks Beach. He could see daylight. Then, he saw the two mothers standing cheek by jowl, talking furiously. His troubles weren't over yet.

Delores called him over to the garden. When he got there, his father slapped him on the back.

"We're all very proud, Son."

"Thanks, Dad. But you might want to save it."

Peter pointed to Theresa and Rose Ann.

"We still have a couple of humps to get over."

"Son, it's like the Army. Just go where they tell you."

Delores dropped her cigarette butt on the ground, stamping it with her high heel.

Why this bothered Peter, he couldn't say.

"C'mon, Delores, on church grounds?"

"Since when are you Mr. Holy Roller? Besides, you think the priests don't smoke. Please, they're like chimneys."

"You sound like your mother."

"I can't compare. You wouldn't believe what she and your mother-in-law are up to now."

"Do I want to know?"

Pasquale squeezed Peter's shoulder.

"No, Son, you don't. I'll only say it has something to do with Evelyn's father. Tell you the truth, I feel for the poor S. O. B."

"Don't worry, Brother, I'm sure you'll get all the details from Evelyn. In fact, there she goes."

Evelyn and her bridesmaids were walking slowly to the back entrance of the church.

"Shouldn't we be inside?" Peter wondered aloud.

Pasquale took a final drag on his cigarette, and put it out against a tree.

"If I know your mother, they'll call you as soon as they want you. And don't forget about the Pope. He's got a whole crew to get ready. That takes time."

If Peter's nerves were near an edge, Delores was there to push them closer to it.

"Do you at least have the ring?"

"That's one thing I didn't forget. I can even describe it for you in technical terms."

"No, wait till I get mine. I'll bet you right now — drinks for a month — my rock'll be bigger."

If Delores knew what she was in for when the time came for her ring, she'd be grateful for the pity Peter was beginning to feel. The next moment they all heard the front door of the church fly open and slam shut. Evelyn, alone, came charging toward them. Peter had assumed she hadn't seen them on her way in, but then when it came to the religious ceremonies of his life, he'd assumed many things, almost all of which assumptions God had taken extra care to prove wrong.

Delores couldn't help herself.

"Uh-oh! You know you're not supposed to see her today, right?"

"We woke up in the same bed this morning."

Pasquale crossed himself.

Evelyn was in tears. Peter held up a finger and walked toward her.

"What happened?"

As they walked toward the street, Evelyn's thin frame shook with sobs.

"She's making this too hard. Get in the limo."

They got in the bridal limo, whose driver Peter signaled to wait outside for a few minutes.

"What is it?"

"My mother. She struck."

"Struck what? Struck how?"

"Struck my wedding day. She's trying to change everything. I told her last week my father might be in town, and he would want at least to walk me to my Uncle Nunzio's side when we go down the aisle."

"Did I know that?"

"It doesn't matter. He's my father, and I didn't want you to worry."

"I wouldn't have worried. Now I'm worried."

"Anyway, today she informs me she doesn't even want him in the church. And he's been calling all morning. On top of that, she's changed the seating. Now all the aunts and uncles she's close to are sitting up front, and all the ones I spend the most time with are in back. And then she changed the menu. No more empanadas. She thinks your family won't eat them, because they won't know what they are."

"That's never stopped my family before."

"So I told her I'm not getting married in the church."

"What? Honey. Wait. Remember, the Pope's inside."

"He'll keep. And I told my mother, and I'm telling you, that I'll only get married now if it's at the beach."

"The beach?"

"On the beach."

"What did she say?"

"She bit the side of her hand."

"Wow. What did my mother say?"

"It's funny. It didn't seem to bother her. She even volunteered to tell the Pope."

Peter wanted to be surprised, but wasn't.

Theresa narrowed her eyes.

"So I'm going to the beach. And I don't care who else comes."

"Is the Pope coming?"

"If they still want this to be a Catholic thing, he'd better."

"What should I do?"

"Stay here, so you can get everybody else to move. They'll feel sorry for you."

For a moment Peter considered hopping in the driver's seat, locking the doors, and kidnapping his bride. Then he understood what he had to do. Now that they had dragged themselves this far, it wouldn't take much to convince everyone to travel a little further to see such a historic event. So the Pope would be the whole game. He would be Ohio in a Presidential election. And when it came to campaigns, Peter's mother was in a class by herself.

But it was Marcello, monitoring the proceedings, who broke the news. Upon hearing it, the Pope felt a series of emotions. The first was regret. Was this indeed his reward? The culmination of a life devoted to castigating and sometimes retaliating against passionate but politically oblivious liberation theologists; a life dedicated to carrying out the orders of superiors who distrusted his own placid demeanor and his ineluctable Deutschtum? When he recalled his many years of solitary study; the effort he had poured into a dissertation on Saint Bonaventure (a humble professor attacked by other professors for his writing; a man who re-wrote history in the interests of strengthening the Church; and, it had to be admitted, a diplomatic functionary, whose greatest miracle was the perfect posthumous preservation of his own head); when he recalled his time of toil as professor of theology and university administrator; his quiet, tireless work for Cardinal Frings on Vatican II; his time-consuming editorship of a journal read by only a few hundred especially bored deacons; his lengthy Bavarian bishopric (with the impossible motto "Cooperators of the Truth"); his work on the new Catechism; his deanship of the College of Cardinals; and finally, all his sub rosa maneuvering to attain the exalted rank he now somewhat less than enjoyed, he had to question his motivation. For all Bonaventure's efforts, the man had been poisoned. Ah, what peace of mind and pleasure had both this Pope and the saint forsaken in leaving the academy.

Then it occurred to the Pope that although his own pleasures were of a more demanding nature, they were still pleasures yielding immediate results and immediate gratification, in the form of the joyful faces and light hearts of all those faithful who saw in his presence the hope for a greater life beyond the poverty he knew that they would never escape — and, he often felt, would be better off, for their own and the church's sake, not to. Which thought brought him contentment warming to his old bones as the Florida sun. His own parents, after all, had lived from more tedious labor: his father, a policeman; his mother, a cook. The rest of the family had been farmers. And although the Pope had in his youth been proud of his physique and stamina, he had always been afflicted with lower back problems resulting from curvature of the spine. He could not actually fathom a life in which the Lord would have seen fit to have him harvest turnips or milk Holsteins for his livelihood. His rewards in fact were great, even if they required him to exist half of the time as a personaggio, the sort of character his forbear had loved to play.

A cameraman flashed by the open door of the lounge, bringing the Pope a sense of acceptance with just a tinge of anger with himself, and fear. He would have to go to the beach, because he himself had insisted on this wedding as a media event. On second thought a beach ceremony could enhance the program. It could be presented as a subtle "Spring Break with the Pope." And he might use the occasion to relax the rule about marriages having to take place inside of church buildings. At a minimum he could make exceptions for marriages performed by the Vicar of Christ, and perhaps for his archbishops. This precedent — coming in the form of a decree or privilege —

would also simplify the logistics of the papal marriage tour. Henceforth, he might, if he chose, marry a couple who would then parachute from a plane over the Outback, or perhaps dive from a pier on a sparsely populated Caribbean island. Once he had broken through the fourth wall, so to speak, the possibilities would be endless. The Pope felt better now, energized. At that very moment, in the doorway appeared the large mother in the purple dress. And in that anxious instant, he acted as any rational man would. He opened his arms to her, and put up no resistance whatsoever.

††
†

The relentless afternoon sun had nearly cleared the public beach at Treasure Island. Evelyn sat on a bench near the bathhouse, still in her wedding dress, facing a playground in the white sand. Two well-placed palm trees shaded her. Ice cubes she had bought on the way, held a few at a time on the back of her neck, kept her cool enough to wait. She was used to waiting. For this day, or an easier version of this day, she had waited longer than most women. She could wait a little longer, the way she would have to wait for a child. When their little boy or girl was old enough, they'd visit her family and stay out here, bring the child to this playground, and later tell him or her who in the family to watch out for. But at this point she and Peter would probably have to adopt, which is where having the Pope involved, and at the mercy of Peter's mother, might come in handy. A girl no older than three was staring at her from the top of the curly slide, the way the girl's parents were staring from a facing bench. Normally this would bother her. But something had changed. Why should she care? What difference would it make if she did? After all this, was a dirty look something she couldn't handle? Was it going to knock her off track? She watched the little girl stomp her feet and wave her hands in the air. Then, as she watched her slide, Evelyn heard the screeching of tires. Through the breezeway, she saw the first limo parked, and several more motoring into the lot at what seemed like uncalled-for rates of speed. Holding her train, she walked out to meet the party, led by Peter, who looked now like a general, striding upright, beaming, gung-ho. When he reached Evelyn, he gave her a huge hug, lifting her off the ground, then picked her up and carried her onto the beach. Half-way across the quarter-mile stretch to the Gulf, he was sweating like an animal, but remained all smiles.

"I love you more than ever," he said.

Evelyn kissed him passionately, pulling away when she felt his knees buckle a bit.

"Why?" she asked.

"Because you wanted to come here."

She squeezed him again, and over his shoulder watched the small army of their relatives and friends crowd around the concession stand.

"Where's the Pope?

"Don't worry. He's here, in the limo, planning."

"Doesn't he already know how the marriage is supposed to go?"

"Sure, but there are a few minor problems to solve."

At a rental stand near the lifeguards, Peter lowered Evelyn to the sand. He drew money from his pants pocket — glad now he had followed his father's advice always to carry a wallet, even on his wedding day — and paid for an umbrella and two chairs. He planted the umbrella a few yards from the waves, and helped Evelyn settle on her temporary throne. The water was calm. Pelicans swooped and bobbed. A few hundred yards offshore a pod of dolphins broke the surface, their dorsal fins flashing as they rose and fell like carousel horses.

"What happens now?" she asked.

"Well, first the Pope has to write some kind of decree about where we're getting married. To make that work, he has to consecrate some kind of structure here."

"The closest thing is the bathhouse, and, I'm sorry, I'm not getting married there."

Evelyn kicked the sand. Peter took her hand.

"I know, I know," he said. "But have a little . . . Do I need to say the word?"

Evelyn screwed up her face.

"And remember, we have two secret weapons."

Rose Ann was happy with herself now, happy that she'd read Theresa right. She was a little powerhouse, all right. When Evelyn walked out, she'd been right there for Rose Ann the whole way, on the same line of the same page. Now that they'd reached the beach, and all the aunts and uncles had snacks to tide them over, they could think about the Pope and what he needed. She knew all along her daughter wouldn't go for blessing a bath-house or a cabana, so her first thought was to have the Pope bless one of the little hotels. Trouble was none of them was all that close to the water. On her way out of the church, Evelyn had specifically yelled something about the water's edge. She ran this line of reasoning by Theresa, as they both ate soft-serve ice cream cones at a picnic table. They could see the bride and groom's umbrella in the distance.

"You see them there?" Theresa remarked. "Clear heads. Like they don't have a care in the world."

"At least they have an umbrella. With that sun, my daughter's liable to completely ruin that wedding dress. And believe me, she drove me crazy find-ing it."

"My son doesn't even own that tuxedo. Watch, he'll wind up having to buy it. Or, if he's as poor as he usually is, I will."

Theresa noticed a few umbrellas, all yellow, scattered along the beach.

"Where did they get their umbrella?"

"Oh, the rental. Right down there."

A little while later Theresa was leading a barefoot wedding party march across the beach, then handing the lifeguard two crisp one hundred-dollar bills. In return the lifeguard handed her all the umbrellas left in the rack, twenty or so, which she distributed to Pasquale and other able-bodied mem-bers of the party.

"Set them up there, behind that one," she instructed, her voice rousing Peter and Evelyn from their respite. They stood up and turned to see what looked like a group of yellow turtles crawling toward them. As they watched, their family and friends arranged the umbrellas to form a patchwork tent.

"That's it," Theresa called out. "Right there. And I need all the brides-maids and groomsmen to move back to that grass over there. Now somebody go get the Pope."

The Pope was rankled. His linen vestments, for which, at Marcello's behest, he had stood through an interminable session with the Vatican tailor, were not breathing as anticipated. He was further bothered when he spotted the raft of umbrellas and the bridesmaids standing near a beach volleyball net. This was a wedding, not a picnic. Noting his disturbance, Marcello reassured him.

"We can shoot here, Your Grace. In fact, the light will be superb."

"Then we will do what we must. In the end this ordeal may smooth our paths to Heaven."

"One assumes, Your Eminence."

"One assumes nothing, Marcello, except that it is much easier than ever to humble the Pope."

Sweating profusely by the time he did, the pontiff gained the cathedral of umbrellas, and was about to give it a perfunctory blessing, when Marcello approached, to whisper in his ear.

"Unfortunately, Holy Father, we are without the benefit of holy water."

Before answering, the Pope took a moment to regard the Gulf of Mexico.

"As I stand here, my son, gazing out upon this endless sea before us, I must make one of two additional assumptions: either that the day's cosmic joke is indeed on us or that your limited resourcefulness must ultimately thwart your ambition to rise in this venerable institution. May we at least assume that I have a scepter at my disposal."

"Yes, Your Grace."

"Then I have all the water I shall need."

The Pope walked to the edge of the surf, and faced the celebrants. Guglielmo cued the cameras. Practically yelling over the ambient noise, the pontiff addressed his flock.

"Children of God, here in Treasure Island and around the world, we have assembled today, to join these two lovely and faithful young people in holy matrimony. In advance of this joyous endeavor, however, we must, as you are aware, also initiate a practice made official only today by the Holy Church: the ad hoc consecration of a lay edifice as vessel, womb, if you like, of a Catholic union of souls."

As the Pope spoke, a crowd began to gather from up and down the beach, gradually surrounding the umbrella-protected core of celebrants. As they did the Pope spotted a group of men he knew as members of the Swiss Guard, dressed in similar sets of khaki shorts, guayabera shirts and dark sunglasses, jogging toward the shoreline from the concession stand. Their presence confirmed for him that this would not be the poignant ceremony he had envisioned. At least Marcello made sure all cameras remained off the Guard, allowing them time to disperse and mingle. Reasonably certain that a potential assassin would have to be preternaturally clever or mentally handicapped to find him here, the Pope felt as secure as he ever had since taking the job. He continued, lifting his scepter and addressing the audience again.

"Let us pray now for the blessing of this vast sea at my back. I hereby consecrate it, this Gulf of Mexico, and declare it henceforward a body of water holy in the eyes of the Lord. Thanks be to God."

"Amen," the crowd intoned, as the Pope faced the sea and waved the scepter across its turquoise vastness, appearing on camera as a magician atop a painted proscenium stage. Marcello then walked to the water's edge and filled a small plastic drinking-water bottle, the only kind handy, with the salt water of the gulf. Handing the bottle to the Pope, Marcello moved off camera again, as the Holy Father, apparently conscious of the corrosive power of seawater, gingerly poured some over the end of his scepter, which he then shook in benediction over the umbrella cathedral.

Pasquale craned his neck, to see over one of the uncles from the Mafia chart. Theresa stood at his side, cradling in her right hand a miniature Infant of Prague, equally rapt in the goings on. Keeping his eyes fixed on the Pope, Pasquale spoke in a dreamy tone.

"Oh, he's doing some job up there. What do think, Terry? Will they show this on the Catholic channel?"

"How many times do you have to watch it, Pattelli? Once your son's married, that's that."

After reading from the Gospel ("Blessed are you when they insult and persecute you," a passage he had always found helpful in dealing with church politics), the Pope then called up Evelyn's father. As it turned out, Evelyn and her mother, through a third party, had negotiated a settlement in which

her father, instead of walking her part way to the altar, would hug her at the
very end of the procession, and get to do the first reading (of Rose Ann's
choosing). This arrangement would unfortunately knock Evelyn's ancient
Aunt Mamie, whose eyes were so bad — God bless her — she could barely
read anyway, out of the spotlight. The reading, listed in the The Rite of Marriage as "In his love for Rebekah, Isaac found solace after the death of his
mother," ended with the lines,

> Then Isaac took Rebekah into his tent;
> he married her, and thus she became his wife.
> In his love for her Isaac found solace
> after the death of his mother Sarah.

Evelyn, waiting out of sight near the volleyball court, but still from the
distance able to follow her father's mellow baritone, couldn't believe what
she was hearing. Her sister Michelle, bridesmaid, and always ready to mock
their parents, stood by her side.

"God, listen to that," Evelyn grumbled.

"I know," Michelle answered. "Your mother's been talking about her
death since I was five years old."

The next voice they heard was the Pope's He stood erect, his chin thrust
out, Peter couldn't help thinking, like Mussolini.

"This sacrament of matrimony is to us the Lord's most precious earthly
gift. To have by one's side a helpmeet is the greatest joy of all — as no doubt
our young Peter, having himself nearly taken holy orders and chosen the life
of restraint expected of all God's representatives on earth, will soon discover.
That is why I have chosen to come here, to a land normally associated with
exotic animal tours, hedonistic getaways, and a man's declining years, to cel-
ebrate, as I will this year in many parts of the world, a single union in Christ.
Even in those places that to us seem modern-day Sodoms, these single unions
are the wellsprings of earthly happiness and the bedrock upon which we
build a godly society and strong church."

Expecting at least some applause for that final line, the Pope felt the need
to pause here, for effect, and to improvise.

"For what is society and what is the church but all of you, all of us?"

A few of the gawkers clapped tepidly. The Pope was left to console himself. If these two families were so star-struck or moribund as not to respond to his rallying call, at the very least he could imagine that their silence would allow for an excellent audio track. He looked to Marcello, who, wishing now he had talked the pontiff into guitar accompaniment, signaled the organist.

Michelle smoothed the front of her dress.

"This is us, Sis."

As she took Uncle Nunzio's arm, Evelyn pushed her bare toes deep into the warm, powdery sand. She would remember the sensation as the feeling of being with a good man. When she reached the front row, she looked over at her mother, whose expression said one word: "Hallelujah!"

Beside the leader of the Catholic Church, waiting for her, was Peter. As he stood there, she could picture him in the papal outfit. A lime green or even beige robe would suit him best. Peter, for his part, winked at his parents. In response his father dabbed his eyes with a handkerchief, while his mother pointed for him to pay attention to the Pope, who was beginning to wilt in the heat and humidity.

"You may all now enjoy a moment of repose," he said, surreptitiously fanning himself as the audience found a new equilibrium.

In such a setting, at such a moment of discomfort for all, the Pope thought is best not to showboat. Indeed he would fall back on the bit of advice that he had gathered in his hotel room, from the cable television station for sporting events: Act as though you have been there before. He asked the couple their intentions in simple language, requested that the ring be brought forth posthaste, and watched as they sealed their marriage with a passionate kiss — briefly recalling, as he did, his own adolescent infatuation with Fraulein Schweinsteiger, the Austrian belle of Traunstein. With the couple still before him, he offered the nuptial blessing, of which Peter noticed only the lines, "Father, you have made the union of man and wife so holy a mystery that it symbolizes the marriage of Christ and his Church." Peter's bride in fact was mysteriously pensive, her lips drawn down, her gorgeous forehead and cheeks smooth as the sky.

Once he'd dispensed with the Lord's Prayer and with the Eucharist, improvised from several loaves of Cuban bread, the Pope turned to the audience.

"Now," he began, "I would like especially to bless the parents, in particular the mothers of the bride and groom, who have, through their astonishing attention to their children and to the function of the Holy Church in their lives, made it possible for us to do the Lord's work."

In the wake of the Apostles' Creed, Theresa wondered what she would do with herself now that her son would proabably soon move to Florida with this wife. Delores was still a long way from giving her grandchildren, and Pasquale was more worried about his workshop than about how they would spend their golden years together. Golden years? Who was kidding who? Studying Marcello as he took the Pope's scepter and walked over to speak with the organist, Theresa hit on an idea. If it weren't for her, this whole thing would've fallen apart. How would the Pope be able to do this all over the world without her help? That was it. She was going on tour with him. When they got home, she'd make Pasquale zuppa di mussels, and break the news, over demitasse.

Pasquale just then, like Rose Ann across the sandy aisle, was preoccupied with logistics. There was a nice breeze now, and the sun was setting. Maybe they could eat here on the beach. But where would they all do the tarantella?

Meanwhile, in his head the Pope was modifying his grand plan. To continue with these weddings, he would have to summon an archbishop or two, as well as a team of Vatican writers. The writers would consult with all future couples in scripting ceremonies down to the letter. The archbishops would handle the lion's share of duties, that he might simply preside. To the weary cleric, the truth was clear: At his age, he would be best off observing marriage from afar.

"*In nomine Patris, et Figlii, et Spiritus Sancti.*"

Peter and Evelyn, face to face, grasped each other's arms, while the Pope droned on with his final blessing and their families talked amongst themselves. Evelyn slid her hands up Peter's sleeves and gently pushed his jacket from his shoulders, letting it fall to the sand. Then she reached for the hasp of her train, which Peter helped her undo. It too fell free. The Pope saw nothing of this, his arms upraised and face lifted to the ether. The heads of most of the crowd were bowed, so that only the Swiss Guard and a few others noticed as Evelyn led Peter into the gulf. They walked hand and hand, up to their waists in the clement water. Peter looked to the heavens. A few thunderheads were rolling in from the south, promising rain. He wrapped his arms around Evelyn's waist, drawing her close. As they kissed, from the corner of his eye Peter saw a line of their loved ones on the shore, the mothers in the lead, waving and calling out well wishes unintelligible from here. Behind them, his hands on his hips, stood the frowning Pope. The couple waved back and, without speaking a word, waded deeper into the holy body.

THE IMBECILE PROFESSOR
(A STUDENT'S DEFENSE)

Throughout your childhood your parents, both respected academicians, barely speak to you, because you can not hold up your end of a conversation on the use of insect as symbol in the work of German-language writers other than Kafka; and because you neither respond to external stimuli like powerful beams of light shone directly in your eyes, nor form complete sentences until the age of twelve. In high school you flunk special education courses, because, in your misunderstood protest against corporate influence in the classroom, you refuse to comprehend short essays on television stars and miracle appliances of the future. When the time comes to attend college, you are denied entry by your own conscience and other people's jealousy of your intellect, whereupon you begin writing your thoughts on the blank sides of dismantled biscuit boxes. You show this work to your parents, who dismiss it as the indecipherable scribbling of an idiot. They then contemplate comparing you to Doestoevsky's Prince Myshkin, in a collaborative, interdisciplinary, scholarly paper.

Unbowed, you continue your misread (until now) writings, developing a unique system of hieroglyphics. You spend twenty years sitting on the floor of your parents' basement, their television bringing you images of America in turmoil. You write the most trenchant social commentary of the century. You rock back and forth. Your rocking grows more violent, as your thoughts become more complex and intense. Your aging parents ignore the metronomic cogitations of a rare genius. They commit you to an institution.

Now, with little hope of ever publishing your brilliant life's work, you pass your spare time pressing your face against the eight-by-twelve reinforced glass window of a door separating your ward's exercise area from the visitors' waiting room. You believe the visitors waiting on yellow vinyl couches are waiting for your message. You despair.

Then one day an alert young visitor hears your grunting through the door and looks up to see you holding your latest manifesto to the window.

††
†

This is how I discovered him.

The moment he lowered the first Delphic biscuit box, I turned to the attending nurse.

"Who is that man?"

"That one is called Hugh," she answered, bland as milk. "Hugh Canot."

"Hugh," I repeated, ravishing the name with my lips, staring into those soul-piercing eyes.

Before leaving that day, I requested a visit with Hugh. On the request form, under "Reason for Visit," I wrote in sloppy block lettering I knew no busy administrator would bother to decipher, "INQUIRY." Under "Relationship to Resident," I wrote, "STUDENT."

To our first interview I brought a notepad, Hugh a foot-high stack of flattened biscuit boxes bound with an enormous green rubber band. (The rubber band with Hugh's original ink smudges remains in my possession.) Across the small desk stationed between us, Hugh handed me the boxes one at a time. Intrigued and baffled by his code (in good company in so being), but curious, I held the first box up and pointed to the first line. Hugh immediately began pronouncing the symbols for the next several hours. I took notes until my wrist ached.

By the end of our sixth interview, I had compiled what amounted to a new language, the complexity of which American civilization had never known. By this time Hugh, always (like me, I must admit) frail and unkempt from neglecting the pleasures of food and vanities of grooming for the rigors of serious thought, showed signs of severe fatigue. At our seventh interview, reduced to a near-comatose state by his accelerated work schedule and by prescription narcotics intended to numb him and his colleagues to institutional life, he extended a trembling hand bearing the most recent few of what I dubbed his "Biscuit Prophecies." Mouth and tongue lolling, face expressionless and bloated, eyes hollow and grave as curses, he placed the boxes before me and clasped my hand in his. He grunted, squeezed my fingers, and implored me with all the pent power of a neglected oracle, "Make my words known" [translation mine].

I yanked my hand away, saluted him, and swore, "The world will hear you."

In giving me the gift of his life's work, Hugh had given me the gift of mine. I would be Hugh's voice, his follower, his bulldog. Months passed as night and day I pored over the manuscript. The work of translation exhausted me, but I slept my few hours each night, content because immersed in the truths of our time.

The following are excerpts from the manuscript. I print transliterations of Canotian Code on the left, and on the right corresponding English translations (Numbers in parentheses following the excerpts indicate biscuit box and line.)

"Se nyod Merne woh es."
(1, 3)

"The beauty of America is a dream of itself."

"Mer uh boh dat oh-oh uh woo dat boh uh Merdey woo uh oh-oh dat."
(5, 17)

"Men love women as Americans love the world. Women love men as the world loathes America."

"Pow deynin no wee oh-oh Merne wan."
(52, 34)

"In America it takes one man to succeed, but an entire nation to fail."[1]

Having finally translated the 8,721 biscuit boxes Hugh had to that point filled, I felt a great sense of relief mingled with anxiety. I lay in bed night after night, day after day, wondering how to make public the private insights

---

[1] There has been some dispute over the final excerpt above, as "oh-oh" may sometimes without alteration be used to represent the plural—usually "oh-oh dey oh-oh."

that might forever change the way we understand ourselves. Then one afternoon I rolled over and seized from the nightstand a picture of me and Hugh in the visitors' room of the institution, the complete stack of "Biscuit Prophecies" towering between us. He had been incarcerated for five years now. His precious thought would die with him behind walls of soundproof glass, cinder block, and reinforced steel, because the work alone would never suffice. Even if someone in the myopic world of publishing were to have a lengthy enough flash of intelligence to publish and promote "The Prophecies," they would never be accepted as a coherent philosophy of modern life, without the cachet of authorial mental impairment. The world needed to see Hugh, to know his struggle. I needed Hugh in the flesh. Hugh needed me. And Hugh's parents, the very people who had condemned him, held the key to his freedom and our success.

The Canots' phone number was unlisted, but it was simple enough to track the couple down through their academic department. The department secretary was more than happy to share with me their contact information, address, record of personal hygiene, and other details of their private lives. Ernst and Cassandra Canot lived in a swank neighborhood at the edge of town, apparently in perpetual dishabille. They shunned students, and never asked after colleagues' health or family. Persuading them to free Hugh would prove a daunting task; still, persuading them would be easier than persuading myself to abandon Hugh to obscurity. I rang the Canots, and, in the guise of a former high school classmate sympathetic to Hugh's condition, arranged a meeting, to discuss their son's fate.

The Canots enjoyed all the luxuries a semi-retired academic couple could afford. Their mediocre scholarship and slapdash lesson plans had garnered them a lovely four-bedroom "cottage" in the English style, overlooking the river valley of which their college town was the hub. Since Hugh existed now as a ward of the state, the money they saved from not having to feed, clothe, and bathe him paid for their country cabin, to which they escaped on weekends. This was one of the first pieces of information Mr. Canot divulged, after mentioning how lucky I had been to catch him on a rare springtime Saturday in town.

"A friend of Hugh's then?"

"I used to look out for him."

"You know what's happened, I suppose?"

The air was humid, uncomfortable. Mr. Canot fidgeted in his iron patio chair, then drained a gin and tonic.

"Cassie, the pitcher!"

Cassandra Canot had been sitting indoors, at her kitchen table, ostensibly finishing an overdue article for the alumni newsletter. But now, answering her husband's call, she arrived dressed in a thin robe, holding the lime-scented pitcher in one hand and her own highball in the other. She placed the pitcher on the iron table, plopped down in an iron chair, sighed, and began ignoring our conversation. Mr. Canot spoke again.

"Hugh was not the kind of boy many people would understand."

"Yes, I know," I agreed.

"Yes, yes."

"He never spoke much in school. I always wanted him to join my salon, but alas, he never gave me an answer."

"No, no, Hugh was more given to his grunting . . . but excuse me, young man, what was your name again?"

"Albert, Sir, Albert Terico."

"What is it you want to ask, Albert, about Hugh?"

"As I mentioned on the phone, Sir, I visited him recently."

"Yes," he said through a cupped hand, "you knew him in high school."

"That's right."

"Yes, well, we weren't aware Hugh had friends."

Ernst Canot reached for his cocktail and threw back the last mouthful before refilling the glass.

"It's true, Sir. As I said, I helped him. Of course, Hugh kept most things to himself."

The sound of ice melting and collapsing inside the pitcher prompted Mr. Canot to refill his glass and take another drink. Cassandra Canot continued staring into space.

"Sir, when I visited him," I confessed, "Hugh showed me his writing."

"His scrawl," Mrs. Canot, suddenly revived, interjected.

"With Hugh's help," I continued, "I determined that this 'scrawl' was actually an ingenious code. To be brief, Mr. and Mrs. Canot, I believe your son's writings are extremely important. I want to help publish them, publicize them. But I need your help. I need your permission to check him out of the institution."

My proposition drew the eyes of both Canots from their drinks.

"Excuse me again, young man," Mr. Canot said sternly, "but why should my wife and I allow someone we don't know to take our son from the only place where he can be properly attended?"

"It would only be for a certain time," I replied, "and I could take care of all his personal needs, or, if you like, we could stay here."

Mrs. Canot sank in her chair and began sobbing.

"Albert," Mr. Canot said, the pitch of his voice rising, "I'm afraid you'll have to leave now."

"If you insist, Sir, but it's a shame."

"That's right, my boy, it would be a terrible shame for our son to be exposed to the world's cruelties."

"It's only that. . . . It's just that there would be a great deal of money involved. Enough money to give your son the best care available — in a home of his own."

Mrs. Canot dried her eyes.

A half-hour later I had the Canots' permission and blessing. Hugh and I would begin our campaign.

Some might call him an idiot savant or perhaps autistic, but I believe otherwise. Hugh could share the pleasure he obviously derived from his work. Day and night, as I sent off manuscripts and phoned publishers and agents, Hugh sat in a corner of my apartment happily stuffing his mouth with biscuits, pulling apart the boxes, continuing his mission. His grunting took on gleeful tones. My translations of Hugh's prose allowed me to speak his code, so that once we grew comfortable with each other we were able to discuss any subject: from the merciless degradation of the Great Plains to the magnetic polarity of New York to the fashion gulf between intellectuals and the general public.

"Ba-ba-ba-ba, blee Merne tree-tree coo-coo foo weet? ["Do woodcocks sing in the American forest before four a.m.?"], he asked me one evening.

"Na Merne tree-tree foo weet" ["In the American forest, nothing sings"], I replied.

I did little of my own writing during this period, satisfied as I was to secure Hugh's legacy. It took several months to sell any publisher on the idea that he or she could make an easily misconstrued book into a bestseller, by marketing it as the first book conceived and completed entirely by a clinical moron. (Several publishers in their complacency claimed to have already published such books.) By the end of the year, *The Collected Biscuit Prophecies* had been scheduled for publication in America by the Alaska State University Press and in Europe by a consortium of publishers who had decided to distance themselves from any revolutionary response to the book by presenting it with an illegible imprimatur.

Our book tour began on February 29th, in the village of Smartantusk, in Central Alaska. Hugh and I decided that he would not speak during readings and signings. Such mundane duty would fall to me, while Hugh would focus on cultivating an enigmatic presence. That night on the tundra, the mercury dropped to 97 degrees below zero (discounting wind chill), but several people showed up, having had, I suppose, ample free time to read *The Prophecies* cover to cover. We selected one of Hugh's favorite prophecies, one of the earliest, a metaphorical piece on the permanent sunset of American power (distinct from American culture, which, Hugh and I agreed, deserved a metaphor all its own). As I read, the gathered Alaskans tacitly approved. Hugh, noting this, tacitly thanked them — a brilliant touch.

If the reading gave the audience a Canotian worldview, it was the signing afterward that turned them from readers into devoted students of "Professor" Canot, as we would come to know him.

Not content to sign copies of *The Prophecies* in his usual code, Hugh extemporized a new one for the occasion, guiding my hand to make marks on flyleaves, which the fortunate recipients would spend the most fulfilling months of their lives interpreting. On one copy Hugh wrote,

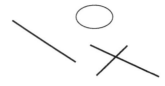

On another,

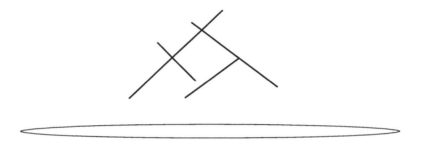

And on a third, he composed what would prove one of his most difficult, most scrutinized lines:

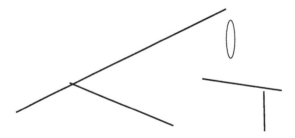

Academies full of scholars and students have since attempted translations, but without clues — which, for reasons he had, I'm certain, thought through carefully, Hugh refused to provide — they have struggled to cut a path of simple meaning through this dense jungle of rumination.

From that first venue, Hugh and I allowed the winds of acclaim to carry us onward to Fairbanks, Juneau, and Nome. In the last of these polar capitals, two hundred cerebrally ravenous Nomics packed the Grizzly Cup to hear me share Hugh's words. The surpassing beauty of his spoken language infused his expostulations on America's lost beauty with such power that the crowd nearly rioted. This incident — now known as "The Alaskan Eruption" — began when a young woman in the audience claimed that the haunting and suggestive line,

> "Clikne mi poof dat woo woh," (19. 99)
>
> "The beauty women held has vanished forever into silicon(e),"

had anti-womanist overtones.

Immediately, another parka-clad young woman standing at the back of the room sprang to her feet and yelled, "No! Canot is with us!"

A melee ensued: diatribes, barbs, and hurled folding chairs. Seated in a corner, Hugh rocked out the storm. I suffered only contusions and one major challenge from an old man who smelled of salmon.

"Why don't you let the author speak for himself, son? Who are you?"

Appearing to rise as one, the audience united behind these questions. Of course, I could offer no answer — at least none that a simple audience would understand. Hugh himself would never deign to address such a mob, but if he would, would address them bravely, without translation. Misreadings be damned!

I was Hugh and Hugh was I. No one should have wanted or needed to know my history. For that reason, I suppose, the brouhaha over my identity persisted. When we arrived at a Seattle bookstore for our first reading in the Lower Forty-Eight, the throng assaulted us with questions about the trivia of my life. While management succeeded in quieting them for the duration of the reading, they could not contain the post-performance interrogation. As we made our way to the exit, several members of the audience brayed unintelligible demands.

In the meantime a few letters to the editor of *The Nome Intelligencer* were picked up by the wire services and transformed into a story about a "disabled" or "handicapped," or "imbecile" author, the language depending upon the editor's particular fears. At our next reading, the crowd shouted me off the stage.

Facing a wall and gnarling, Hugh steadfastly refused to pander or give way. I thought it best for security reasons to have him led out, after which I managed to read most of the way through one piece he had fortuitously titled "America Hears Only Its Own Voice." Had those limited minds there gathered comprehended half of it, I believe I would, by myself this time, have faced a second Alaskan Eruption.

Fortunately for Hugh and for me, the uproar over his silence and my speech only fueled demand for *The Prophecies*. Within a year it went through three printings. There was talk of a Middle Eastern tour. Then, however, the monumental acclaim cast a dark shadow.

Groups of protestors barricaded the entrances to our reading venues. Activists held aloft poster-sized photos of Hugh rocking in a folding chair. They also held up poster-sized photos of my face surrounded by question marks. In the streets they chanted, "Hoax! Hoax! Hoax!" The name Albert Terico wasn't enough; they demanded my life.

Pusillanimous sponsors canceled our readings one by one. Hugh and I feared that without our voice the public might horribly misinterpret *The Prophecies*. We agreed that I must be heard and that Hugh must remain a mystery. We agreed also that my life, so long as Hugh existed, should never become the story.

Back at my apartment, Hugh and I questioned ourselves. What would be the righteous path? How could we make the world hear us again? Hugh puzzled out answers on a fresh supply of biscuit boxes. I searched for signs between the couch cushions, under the bed, behind the refrigerator, following Hugh's maxims, "Ow-ah vitne crik crik go" ["Follow the crumbs of your life to revelation"] and "Gow itne tee-tee" ["In little things, bigness"]. I found an old girlfriend's bobby pin, a greasy die, the corner of a lost Nietzsche bookmark, and a bosk of wayward body hair. Hugh filled box after box with his code. I read his thoughts, clear as ever — in fact, this clutch of prophecies would later earn the name "The Cartons of Clarity" — but I could draw no conclusions from them. (My own inadequacy before greatness, some would say.) Five weeks into our hibernation, a letter arrived, our first piece of non-bulk mail in over a month. Its brusque language had spilled from the inkwell of Ernst and Dolores Canot.

To Mr. Albert Terico:

As the legal guardians, we receive royalties.
Lawyers possible.
Prefer you write specifics.
Hello to Hugh.

Cordially,

The Doctors Canot

Hugh grunted himself into a lather, then bit off and ate a corner of the letter. Before he could take another bite, I snatched it from him and stared at its meager lines until their sense evaporated and all that remained were characters, marks on a field of bonded rag, anything or nothing. I realized then what we had to do. Hugh pressed his face against the living room window, and I began writing the following letter.

Dear Sirs or Madams,

The public clamor over Hugh Canot compels me to write.

Many readers of *The Collected Biscuit Prophecies*, and others obsessed with Hugh's celebrity, may in months past have heard me read from his philosophical masterpiece — whether it were at their local bookstore, coffee house, or library. Regrettably, regretfully, Hugh and I have had to discontinue our book tour, out of consideration for our sponsors and for Hugh's legacy. We fear that recent protests by those wishing to hear Hugh speak English — which he will never do, as it would compromise his work — I say, we fear these protests will cause irrevocable harm to our sponsors' business.

Protestors have insisted both that Hugh speak and that I divulge the "secret" of my identity. Hugh's silence is not negotiable, rest assured, but, though I feel Hugh and I are one in the work, I will, for the sake of an American public in dire need of our message, recount the insignificant details of my life.

My full given name is Albert Clarence Terico. The first fifteen years of my life hardly matter. I endured the yoke of cruel suburban taskmasters and technocrats, who drove me from a typically anesthetic home to a typically anesthetic center of "education." Of course, there were unpleasant incidents along the way, but none, I believe, worth narrating here.

As the time drew near to apply to our American institutions of "higher learning," I was advised by counselors who refused to understand my early work — essays on the inequities and iniquities of fast food, shopping malls, baseball, and adolescent girls — not to bother applying. Admissions committees would, I had seen, read my application essays and chortle. I refused to yield, however, and adopted the strategy of writing nothing at all, filling the space allotted for essays on "Your Favorite American" or "Your Strategy for Success" with individual hand-printed punctuation marks the size of my right thumb (my favorite mark having been, as I recall, the exclamation point).

Confirming my suspicions of their incompetence, these admissions committees admitted me, one or two offering scholarships. I ultimately accepted an offer from the Alaska State University. There I used my scholarship money to buy food in bulk, which allowed me to remain inside my dormitory room for weeks on end, pondering my future writings and emerging only to attend classes. This system in turn allowed me to graduate with notebooks full of ideas I would pursue when the time came.

After college, I returned to the contiguous ("contagious," as I would often joke) U. S., and continued living as a full-time student (non-matriculated). For two years, I made an independent study of American social mores and their role in driving the clinically insane insane. My mother's psychoses gave me an excuse to visit clinics and institutions under the pretext of exploring new therapies for her (which therapies I have never believed to help the truly deranged or gifted). What remained of my dwindling inheritance allowed me to spend my days recording the results of my studies and sending them to publishers who lacked the training and foresight, and claimed to lack the knowledge of a "viable" market, to accept them. Undaunted, I self-published my work and sold it whenever the opportunity arose, often in the picnic areas of parks. (I suspect some copies remain in circulation.)

My struggle continued to the day I met and recognized the genius of Hugh Canot. Upon reading the first of his Prophecies, I recognized the inferior insight of my own work, and became his student and champion. Today I feel at one with him, and when I speak in public, I speak with his voice.

It is my sincere hope that this autobiography, brief as it may be, satisfy Canot devotees and encourage them to refrain from the distractions of protest and celebrity trivia.

Yours in candor,

Albert Terico

I sent this précis to the editors of every major daily American newspaper. Several papers, including *The Nome Intelligencer,* published the piece, in each case with a misleading preface. *The Intelligencer's* read,

What follows is a letter written by a man who claims to speak for "The Imbecile Professor," who, in spite of his severe mental handicap, himself has made headlines by writing and publishing a book entitled *The Collected Biscuit Prophecies.* We publish the letter here, because its author and "The Professor" have become a popular bookstore attraction, and their book a surprise bestseller. Please be informed that we have not been able to verify that the "protests" to which the author refers actually occurred.

This last line particularly struck me as symptomatic of an American society that is, as Hugh would have said, "oh-ah votz" ["incapable of belief"]. Hugh and I were frustrated, but we waited in the faith that our former sponsors would eventually call. For several days none did. Finally, when we could wait no longer, I wrote a one-line addendum to my previous letter and sent it to the editor of the Nome paper:

Canot will speak in public. I will translate.

The day after the note appeared, a Juneau bookstore called to schedule us. Hugh and I would take our ultimate journey together that week.

We chose to travel the last leg of that journey, from Seattle to Juneau, aboard an antique sailboat. (Hugh deserved a conveyance fit for his imagination.) It was early autumn. The snow hadn't yet advanced down the slopes of the Cascades in the distance. We gazed up at the lightly powdered peaks as our craft, The Cradle, made its way across cobalt Puget Sound.

My father, like Hugh's, had been a recreational sailor, often finishing last in local regattas, but nonetheless devoting most of his time with me as a child to discussing the finer points of tacking and filling. Aboard The Cradle I would manage the sails, while Hugh, when he was physically able and willing to set intellectual work aside, would tie cord around the gunwale pegs. More often he would nestle near the bow in a small dugout meant for equipment. The movement of The Cradle over the waves would satisfy his natural urge to rock. He would sit for six hours at a time, staring at the horizon, while I would tend to the ship's business.

At night inside the cabin, we would plan our course of action. If the public could now accept my translation of Hugh's work, we would ride the wave of our popularity. We would reach out to as many people as we could. Once established, we would seek ever-larger venues. We planned to conclude our American tour with a free reading on The Great Lawn in Central Park. Mind by mind, the nation would change; then, Hugh's thoughts and my voice would set the world right.

In solitary moments, I fretted over our reception. Had the public been satisfied with my published biography? Would they allow me to speak? Could

I express Hugh's profundities in a language they could understand? I regret now ever having entertained these concerns, but at the time they consumed me, and I'm afraid that in my moments of doubt and distraction, I often neglected for great stretches both Hugh and the course we were steering.

The sun was setting in the cabin window one evening, when through the walls I heard Hugh grunting with uncharacteristic fury. As I rose from my bunk, his grunting grew ever higher-pitched. I ran on deck and looked to the bow, just in time to see the soles of Hugh's shoes disappear over the side with an eerily gentle splash. As I clambered forward, I caught sight of Hugh flailing in the water several yards to starboard. I searched for his life preserver. I searched the dugouts, the cabin, the deck under the yardarms. While I rummaged, Hugh was drifting further off. His grunting came now in fits and starts, growing ever fainter, interspersed with gurgles. Desperate, I watched him fight to stay afloat, and then make a pitiful attempt to swim. His eyes on me all the while, Hugh composed himself long enough to point to a spot in the water further astern of him, where visible in the spume were his lost preserver and the giant bundle of manuscript biscuit boxes that never left his sight. Both of these he must have followed into the sea. (A future biographer perhaps will get to the bottom of what happened.)

Hugh flailed, willing himself toward the ruined manuscript of his life's work. For a few moments, I stood silent, lending my will to his. With a final Herculean effort, Hugh succeeding in boarding the manuscript. Seeing this, I grabbed the mainsail arm, and tried tacking in his direction, but just as the craft drew near, a freakish ice floe appeared from nowhere. Although it drifted slowly enough not to stave the hull, it did turn The Cradle broadside to the prevailing winds, driving me further away from Hugh's raft of philosophies.

Fast losing sight of him, I struggled against forces of nature that seemed determined to keep us apart. After what felt like hours, I managed to steer The Cradle back to where I guessed Hugh would be. But when I reached the spot, both he and his preserver were gone. In their place bobbed the bundle of prophecies.

Distraught, I circled the spot, scanning the swells for any sign of life. The bundle drifted by again and again, inky majesty run to blotches of salty sable, dark tears shed for Hugh. With an oar I fished the bundle from the sea, but soon enough, with the descent of total darkness, I let go the man himself. With a heavy heart, I followed my compass to shore.

When I reached Juneau, to my great surprise, the state police were waiting to greet me.

"Good morning!" I shouted, as the sun rose behind a line of uniformed officers perched on the bulkhead like gulls.

They said nothing. When I made land, they boarded The Cradle and meticulously inspected the deck, bridge, and cabin.

"Hugh Canot?" the sargeant-at-arms asked, looking me up and down.

"No," I replied.

The Doctors Canot, it seems, had contacted the authorities back home. With Hugh gone and his manuscript in my possession, I would now be held in their custody, behind a black veil of suspicion.

So here I languish in a sort of Arctic prison, reduced to misery by the idea that Hugh's work will lose its voice, its place in the history of human thought, and its chance to change our race's course. I fear *The Prophecies* becoming brilliant curiosities long forgotten (one day rediscovered?) by a complacent society, remembered only as the work of an "imbecile professor" and his "criminal" accomplice.

Instead of the honorary degrees we had imagined for ourselves, Hugh has been granted oblivion and I, obscurity. Still, I believe in the power of his mind; I feel he will speak through me again. I imagine him rocking on a beach he has gained by tides. He will by now have written with a constant pen some deeper secrets on those biscuit boxes salvaged as the current stole him away. And I can almost read them now, almost tell you what they are.

In Flight

Calvin carried his coffee cup and laptop to the café defined by potted palms and bamboo plants. His plane wouldn't board for at least another forty-five minutes. This would be his first flight since the heightened alerts. He didn't mind the wait. The café flora reminded Calvin of a trip to the Islands with Jennifer, his long-gone, one-time fiancee, a young woman destined for greatness as a film critic. She was five years Calvin's junior, the kind of beauty most people must have thought way out of his league, even though she'd adored him for how gentle, almost childish he was with dogs, and for his dreams of becoming a filmmaker, artist, Renaissance man. Not quite thirty then, he was already producing fifteen-minute documentaries about characters in his Queens neighborhood, such as the retired teacher who resembled and sounded like the actor Christopher Walken, and who once told him as he was walking his chow-chow, "You know, your dog can do many things for you that you aren't aware of." The dog didn't help get him a movie deal, but Calvin was at the time making connections with aspiring producers, and receiving encouraging rejection notices from script agents. Practically every day Jennifer told him that he was on his way.

But Calvin had hidden from her all of his misgivings, the little tumors of doubt that sapped his strength. Jennifer was sharp as a sword. She was confident. She was blond. And she had been raised like so many old-money girls, to assume good outcomes. While Calvin had been raised, like so many working-class boys, to anticipate failure and to make do. Whenever they'd made love, he'd doubted that he'd actually satisfied her, had been powerless to stop himself from asking, "Was it o. k.?", driving her to the conclusion that she too was failing to please.

In fact Calvin had always doubted his gifts. And he never could muster the energy for a move to L. A., where he could better position himself. Jennifer had even offered to go with him. She had been writing book reviews, but could have easily switched to film, her real passion. When Calvin had imagined this move, he'd imagined their story as a bad screenplay, a comedy of errors replete with forced laugh lines, contrived scenes, and an ending that would leave audiences depressed. In her infinite patience, Jennifer had literally taken his hand and proclaimed her undying faith and love for him. She had spoken of children as attractive and confident as she, as ambitious and creative as he. She and Calvin would fill their family home with talk of literature, film, travel and the children's lives. They would slip in and out of bed effortlessly, joyously, banishing assessment and criticism to their proper place outside the bedroom. Years later she'd be able to look back on their life together, and like a good director know she'd been true to her vision. It would instead be Calvin who'd abandon his, out of fear seeking one infatuation after another, until the day he worked up the false nerve to recite to Jennifer a line he'd stolen from an otherwise mediocre film: "I have loved you in my way." It was to be his eloquent exit, but when she'd realized he was dumping her, she'd beaten him bloody with a high-heeled shoe, and sent him careening through the rest of his life.

By the time Calvin got his coffee and sat down in the airport café, the woman he had decided to observe that morning was lost in a gaggle of old biddies winging their way to warmer climes. The first pre-winter chill had set them on the migratory path. Most of them sat with husbands who looked beleaguered but resigned. Were they content, these old men who in their earlier lives had made, as he did now, a habit of following women through public places?

"Marvin, it's your daughter," the magenta-haired woman at the next table told the craggy, balding man who was clearly her husband. She held out a cell phone.

The man grimaced and, slowly, painfully, put down his *Daily News* and stared at his wife for a good thirty seconds before extending a hand to take the call. To give them some privacy, Calvin turned to the floor-to-ceiling window. Outside, a German shepherd was pulling a cop along the tarmac. The dog was sniffing for drugs or maybe plastic explosives. Calvin was growing to hate a world that forced him to associate the loyal dog with terrorism. He turned back toward the tables, and saw half the people around him talking on cell phones. How could the government allow people to fly with all these electronics? No number of German-bred dogs would ever be able to detect the miniscule explosive devices that he was certain clever terrorists could construct. Calvin began to feel that familiar rush in his bowels: one small part the puerile excitement of traveling to a new place, but a much greater part the birthing horror of takeoff and two and a half insipid in-flight movies' worth of suspension high above the Big Blue Marble.

He looked to Marvin and the other old men for reassurance. Many of them had fallen half-asleep. One man kissed his wife's hand. Eighty if he was a day, the man caught Calvin staring. His expression said, *We're on earth for such a short time, what does it matter? So you die in a plane crash. It only hurts for a second.*

Calvin thought he knew what it was almost to die. One night when he was ten years old, he'd watched the broadcast premier of *Logan's Run*. The movie is set in a future world, whose inhabitants at birth have crystals implanted in their right palms. These crystals glow green until their bearers hit thirty, at which point the crystals turn red. To avoid overpopulating a self-contained city built on a platform above the earth's now-barren surface, the authorities arrest all red-crystal people, and send them to an arena, where they are made to death-battle one another with lazers. Those who try to escape are called "runners," and can only survive by first finding a way out of the sealed city and then finding ways to keep themselves alive in the lifeless world beyond. Calvin couldn't remember the ending, but he realized he had already lived eight years longer than the characters played by Michael York and McKenzie Phillips, sexy as she could be in her futuristic white, rayon, low-cut mini-dress, itself rent in an early scene by a guard's lethal beam, the tear exposing her bloody but still very hot midriff. That night as he'd lain in bed watching *Logan's Run*, Calvin had begun to cough. He coughed so long and loud that his father, a hypochondriac, came knocking on Calvin's bedroom door.

"Everything o. k., Son?"

By this time Calvin had hacked up a pint of phlegm into a small garbage can at the foot of his bed. His throat was closing. An hour later his poor, distraught father was carrying his only boy across the parking lot of Mercy Hospital, where Calvin's solemn, pipe-smoking pediatrician had met them, heard Calvin's horrible wheezing, and consigned him immediately to an oxygen tent. Calvin recalled the sensation of a thumb pressing on his throat as he'd tossed and turned inside the plastic bubble, watching his parents' anxious faces distorted by the clear vinyl barrier, unable to speak or to reach out, even to hold his mother's hand. H-type influenza, the doctor had explained, hepatitis of the epiglottis, which sounded like the guy had made it up, but which had almost caused Calvin's heart to stop and the doctor to perform an emergency tracheotomy.

A Rod Stewart video appeared on the giant-screen t. v. in the corner of the airport café: "Some Guys Have All the Luck." A musician friend had told Calvin it was an old reggae song. Rod had probably heard it while on one of his many world tours. God only knew how many flights the man had taken, how much liquor he'd consumed in flight. Alcohol disrupted Calvin's sleep, so, in the hope of getting some elusive mid-air shut-eye, he never drank in airports. He liked the idea, however, of Rod Stewart aloft, stewed, slapping a stewardess's backside, watching old films of himself playing soccer somewhere in Scotland. He wished the man could have frozen his life in 1976.

And there she was again. Now that Calvin looked more closely, she was not one of the prettier women he had ever chosen to watch, and she was just starting, like him, to show a little age. But she appeared to feign the kind of disinterest in opposite-sex attention that Calvin hoped worked for him. They were making the first boarding announcement for Flight 895 to Los Angeles. He watched her as she headed toward the gate, but by the time Calvin crumpled his used napkins and dropped them into his now-cold coffee, she was gone again, boarding breezily with her one bag, simple black dress, alabaster skin, and American smile.

Calvin had no doubt she had passed through security screening with the greatest of ease. Although it was not his fate to have such an easy time of it, he liked the added security, now that it actually seemed to be added. The first couple of years after this all started, he'd had a lot of conversations with friends about the supposedly heightened alert.

"They need those machines," he would conclude, "the ones that x-ray everything."

Such was Calvin's fear that first year that he'd canceled three flights, including a two-hour hop to Cleveland. Who would have suspected a bomb on a flight to Ohio? Exactly!

The only downside to better security was he had to deal with being practically strip-searched each time he flew. His name might look American, but nothing else about him did. His mother was Sicilian, very dark, and his father, as a young man, had had curly black hair. He was usually a suspect. This morning had been no exception.

"Check out Abdul," he'd heard one security guard say to another as he approached in his jeans and beige sport coat, which, at least earlier this morning as he was dressing, had looked appropriate for a trip to Southern California. In front of his bathroom mirror, he'd been remembering the song "It Never Rains in Southern California," dancing around his bathroom in the sleek jacket, pointing at himself in the mirror like a crazed foreign barfly.

"Excuse me, Sir. Could you please step to the side?"

A large man with "TSA" printed on the back of his uniform had led Calvin to an alcove, and asked him to remove his shoes, belt and coat. This had struck Calvin as just the slightest bit unfair, but what had bothered him much more was the idea of omens. His mother had taught all her children to believe in them.

"Are omens good, Mommy?" little Calvin had asked.

His mother had set her finger to her chin and thought about it, then bent down, kissed his forehead and answered, "No, Honey, almost never."

The large man had had Calvin face the wall.

"Where you from?" he had asked, running his hands up the insides of Calvin's tensed legs.

"Brooklyn."

"I mean before that."

"Jersey."

"You speak Arabic?"

"No, you?"

The man had smiled and told him to get dressed and get moving.

Now at the gate, Calvin watched the crew readying the plane that would carry him west. It looked awfully small for such a long trip, but one of the old men seated near him in the waiting area called it "a beauty." Thousands of flights a day: These airlines knew their business. They had to or they'd lose money. Maybe they were losing money.

The call came to board all special-needs passengers and those traveling with children. This was the part that troubled Calvin most, next to zooming up 35,000 feet in a smallish plane: the lines of people waiting to board, all the faces momentarily anxious, with expressions of desperate expectation, but more deeply set, like masks. The word "gulag" came to Calvin's mind. A whole society was complicit in marching its people into thin air. What a great title *The Gulag Archipelago* was. It made him want to read the bulky novel, though he suspected he never would.

His own lack of flair for stirring titles, more than anything else, proved to Calvin that he lacked real creativity and would never write a script worth reading. He'd called his latest "I Snicker at Death." Before that he'd produced "The Man Who Washed Down His Sandwich with a Coke." And last year, worst of all, came "Fish Fry on Fridays." The first few days after sending out these classics, he would be so satisfied with them that he would sing the titles to himself as he walked neighborhood streets. Then for weeks afterward he'd check his mailbox five times a day for the offer of a lifetime that never came.

A stewardess shook Calvin's hand. He didn't like the term "flight attendant," and secretly wished for the emergence of a retro airline, a reminder of the time when air travel smelled more of sex than death. He also didn't like that you could no longer shake the captain's hand. The men (and now women) with the stars and bars were locked away behind bulletproof doors.

23B: neither aisle, nor window. Calvin was doomed to discomfort. Back in the day, you could count on empty seats, a fifty/fifty chance at least one row mate wouldn't show up. To compensate for the packed flights these days, they gave you t. v. and, they claimed, more legroom. An old man, this one wifeless, was making his way down the aisle, chatting up every stewardess he saw, admiring babies, even laughing, as if the whole process were a big joke. The man reminded him of his grandfather, Otis Freinhof, whom Calvin liked better now that he was nearing ninety and living full-time in Florida. Old Otis had a habit of humming to himself. The melodies meandered, and if you asked him what they were, he would answer only, "Bing Crosby." Otis also had a habit of telling his nine grandchildren they should be proud to be American. Calvin wasn't particularly proud to be American, but neither was he ashamed. America had produced a lot of wealth over the years; it had pioneered aviation and music videos; it had also rebuilt Europe and taken in the world's poor, at least some of them, though now it looked like hard choices might have to be made, like the one between national security and cheap landscaping. And America probably had the best-looking women, in terms of variety. Did Calvin really care that Americans seemed fatter and dumber every year? That just made him look better, didn't it? Calvin had never been overly conceited, but in his younger days, he couldn't help railing against ignorant people who did ignorant things such as stab innocent passersby with hypodermic needles as part of gang initiations, or not pick up after their dogs on crowded city sidewalks. He'd grown old enough now not to care, to make not caring a salient feature of his mental make-up.

Calvin avoided in-flight chats. He preferred reading while listening to armrest radio, building a wall between his senses and the ambiance of forced cabin air and turbulence. The old man stopped at Row 23. He looked back and forth from his boarding pass to the number printed between overhead storage bins. Calvin tried to suppress a groan, doubting not for a moment that by the time they touched down in L. A., he would know the names of all the man's grandchildren and of every last one of his Korean War buddies. These thoughts filled Calvin with guilt. Why shouldn't he listen? Weren't they all just trying to get through the trip? If he made it to old age, wouldn't he want someone to talk with on a long flight, aboard which most other passengers would sleep for a while on their companions' shoulders?

"Hiya, Sweetheart," the old man greeted a stewardess trying to squeeze by.

He thrust his boarding pass in her face.

"Where's this seat, dear?

She pointed to Row 25. Calvin exhaled, then reached into his backpack for a novel, and into the pouch in front of him for headphones. When he looked up, his woman was standing there. Her black hair shone like a child's, but her mouth showed the beginnings of wrinkles. Normally in these situations, he felt married even though he wasn't. He felt restrained, fearful. Or maybe the feeling was closer to eighth grade, when in all his callow swarthiness he'd dreamt of asking Annie Langerhans in all her burgeoning blondness to the school dance. But the moment had never been right. He liked to think it hadn't been a lack of confidence in his looks that held him back. He'd just thought he might act prematurely when, if only he could wait, both parties would be less frightened and more prepared for happiness to find them, the way water seeks its level. That was Calvin's story, and yet here stood this woman asking him to pardon her as she brushed past to the window seat. He was suddenly conscious of his own heavy breathing. If she noticed his agitation, she ignored it, taking her seat and opening an issue of *Design for Living*, hiding her dark eyes inside its glossy pages.

"This is your captain, Kurt Gonzalez."

Calvin imagined Kurt Gonzalez as a brown-haired, blue-eyed man whose great-grandparents had come from Mexico to California's Central Valley in the 1920s. His name marked him as "Latino" even if he was more American than Calvin could ever hope to be. If Kurt Gonzalez resented being so marked, you would never know from his chipper, ultra-mainstream p. a. delivery.

"Once you all finish stowing your carry-ons and getting seated, we'll have you off the ground and on your way."

The old couples, the elect who had places in California instead of Florida or Alabama, still standing up, fumbling with their bags and cell phones, held their mouths taut, like bad children trying to keep quiet. Calvin thought of his parents when he'd broken it to them that he would never be a doctor or lawyer, that he would try to be an artist; of how they'd looked as though they were holding live bees in their mouths. They were only mildly assuaged by the news that he would get a master's degree in English and teach until he hit it big.

"Can't you get a real job and do your art on the weekends?' his father had asked.

Maybe he could have, but then how old would be feel by now, and what would he do with all the lucre from whatever practice he should have opened? Weren't the people in first class crying on the inside?

Calvin's woman was looking out her tiny window at the runway and the sun beyond. He seized the moment, turning to stare at her neck and shoulders. He allowed himself ten seconds of fantasy, then fastened his seat belt and tried to slow his breathing with meditation techniques he'd half-learned from a seminar at work. He liked that the college was offering stress-management seminars for all of its employees, but hated that none of the professors ever attended. It was always he and the rest of the support staff, mostly lapsed evangelical office managers, would-be-entrepreneur business-office clerks, or continuing-ed yentas from the far reaches of Brooklyn, who gathered evenings in the faculty lounge, to learn and re-learn the basics of chair yoga, tai chi, and positive visualization. If Calvin had gotten his Ph. D. and become a professor, he would be home in the evenings, home most of the time in fact. He would sit in his underwear at his desk and sip oolong tea; take naps when he needed to; and have plenty of time to write screenplays or at least screen-friendly novels.

He hated himself for this dyspeptic take on co-workers, but why, oh, why hadn't he committed? Instead of leaving for California or going on for the doctorate, he'd left his gig as poorly-paid, part-time English instructor to take the (then it seemed) well-paying position of Publications Coordinator at an obscure arts college in the middle of a decrepit inner-city neighborhood. He'd never imagined how miserable a college administrator could make his life if he missed deadlines for brochures about improved student dining services or faculty silent auctions. Any number of times Calvin found himself sincerely upset by his failure to produce these trivial documents, so upset that he considered introducing whiskey to his work routine, keeping a flask on him at all times, becoming a functioning alcoholic who manages to crank out a single killer script before dying young of organ failure.

Take-off, all things considered, went well. Calvin's tension eased, and he began reading. He read voraciously for nearly an hour, then realized he might be calm enough to sleep or at least lie back and smell her, listen to her flip pages with dainty fingertips. Reclining 23B, he realized that no one had claimed the aisle seat. He was free, and he would exercise his freedom by getting up to pee, now and as often as he liked. He enjoyed airplane bathrooms. They were always next to the food and the stewardesses, all the domestic pleasures of flying bundled together in a cramped gift basket.

He sat on his airborne toilet throne, and thought about the people he would visit: his college roommate Doug and family. He would sleep in one of the kids' rooms, in some town with a possibly specious Spanish name, in a place called The Inland Empire. They would check out the local spot where Doug hosted weekly poetry readings. There would be day trips to Palm Springs, Venice Beach and Santa Barbara. He usually counted on junkets like this one for his share of romantic intrigue. He had met his ex-wife on a business trip to Denver. She had dispelled his false impression that once a woman finds out you're a visitor, she won't get involved beyond a one-night stand. Avril had followed him back to New York, married him, and hadn't borne him any children for several years when she suddenly declared herself a lesbian. Calvin envied her initiative. Since Avril he'd had mostly cocktail, condom and business-card relationships. This week would be worse still, a dull seven days of children, mutual compliments and digital photos. But he'd brought a script along, and a couple of agents' phone numbers. If he could get away for a day or two, he would finally make his move.

When Calvin got back to 23B, she was asleep. Too weary to read and too restless to nap, he stared at the spiked hair in 22B. The hair belonged to a kid with his whole life ahead of him. The flight crew, whose militaristic group tag steeled Calvin's flaccid confidence, began wheeling snack carts down the aisle, one from the front, one from the back. The old men slid upright in their seats. He followed their lead. No sooner did he lower his tray table than he felt the first awful jolt of turbulence. No mere bumps, these were the kind of bungee drops he hadn't even experienced aboard transatlantic flights over godforsaken places like Greenland. Calvin put his headphones on again, only to discover the radio had gone out. He kept them on, and clasped his hands on the armrests. After a few minutes, the air settled. Calvin closed his eyes and, miraculously, fell asleep.

Suddenly the plane was touching down in L. A., in the middle of pastel Wilshire Boulevard. A sea of women filled the sidewalks. All wore sunglasses, which they lowered on their noses as Calvin emerged into the glimmering scene. He wore black – a slim, longer-haired Johnny Cash figure descending a silver staircase. An entourage led him down the center of the street toward a red Lucite stage. The women screamed a name he couldn't make out, though he knew it was his. He raised a hand to acknowledge wave upon wave of applause, gifting a broad smile to the crowd. One face on the sidewalk caught his attention: the face of a five year-old girl atop the body of a stripper. A face he knew. He lowered his sunglasses and squinted hard at the sun-bathed apparition. Sure. It was Tasaliki "Liki" Kafentsis, his kindergarten crush. He waved at her. She locked eyes with him, set hands on puchritudi-nous hips, and with her grotesquely infantile lips mouthed the question, "Wanna play?" A few steps further on, he saw the face of his cousin Lucia, she of the flouncy skirts, dreams of living in a palace, and invitations more subtle than Kiki's. His first taboo love. She danced alone in circles, her eyes almost closed, singing "Freedom" with Richie Havens's voice, at deafening volume. Then the familiar faces flashed fast: his parents' glamourous young tenant, Molly, from Georgia, playing with her cat named Dog; a girl whose name he'd forgotten, whom he'd kissed during the summer of his fourteenth year, while leaning against a campground lakeside boulder; a young woman named Mina Tavares, for whom he'd fallen hard in college, who'd only spo-ken to him once, in Humanities 101, to correct, in front of the entire class, his pronunciation of a character's name from The Iliad, Pa-TRO-klus; and then a lineup of curiously indifferent faces, from his first rich, bipolar girl-friend to the married woman last year who shouted at him, "You're not going to believe this!" in the midst of what she claimed to be her first-ever orgasm. As he climbed the red stage stairs, one of his entourage draped a crimson cape over his shoulders. The crowd roared their approval. He skipped up the last few steps, and skidded over to the mic stand. An orange spotlight hit him full.

"Thank you very much! Thank you!"

A fusillade of cheers struck his skin like a thousand sparks. Each hair on his forearm burst into momentary flame. He savored the sweet smoke. In the street stood a line of helmeted riot police, visors down, arms folded, heads bopping to the crowd's rhythmic chants. The crowd itself had turned to livid confetti, aloft on the charged air. His name echoed all the way to Long Beach and Rancho Cucamonga. When the faces that had witnessed his entrance disappeared, a dazzling blue fog settled in. He felt the moment, raising his arms, to still the delirious throng, then reached into his back pocket and pulled out some rolled up sheets of paper. Whispering a sugary promise in his ear, a raven-haired runway model removed his cape. Ecstatic shrieks rose to the bright heavens. He began reading from his latest screen-play.

Calvin awakened to the smell of her perfume, then felt her hand on his, clenched, pressing down as if his skin were an extension of the seat's Torlon hide. The plane was shaking violently again, lurching, then dropping what had to be a hundred feet.

"Beeeee-Booooo. Beeeee-Booooo."

The "Return to Seat" signs flashed on and off like strobes in a demoniacal discotheque. The crew scurried back to their kitchen posts. The babies on board wailed. The old men pulled their wives closer. Only the sound of Kurt Gonzalez's voice headed off total chaos.

"Ladies and gentlemen, no need for alarm. We've hit a patch of chop. A little severe, but routine. We ask that you remain seated until we're clear."

"Thank God!" one of the old women exclaimed.

Calvin's woman opened her pretty eyes and smiled at him. Then the plane began dipping and bouncing crazily, bucking like a giant tin horse, rolling and skipping sideways. He thought he heard her speak, felt her hand squeeze his. Yes.

"Do your ears hurt?" she whispered, though she appeared to be yelling.

As a matter of fact.

"Yes."

She bit her thumbnail.

"What?" he asked.

"I think it means we're losing cabin pressure."

"Aren't those masks supposed to drop down?"

He leaned in for her answer. By now most passengers were hysterical, the cabin a tempest. For the first time, she looked him full in the face.

"Did you ever think you'd die in an airplane?" she asked in a quavering voice.

In an airplane? No. Blown out of an airplane, hurled from the fuselage. Sure. He was trembling now, almost coughing involuntarily, but trying his best to stay cool.

"No, you?"

She stared through him, squeezed his hand again. Then, as the plane took a plunge that promised to snap it in half, in one motion she raised the armrest between them and pulled his lips to hers. Calvin was conscious of all of himself against all of her: knees on thighs, stomach to stomach, his cheek finding her neck, her teeth nibbling his ear, hands between legs, when she whispered, "Make love to me."

He momentarily raised his head. The passengers had hunkered down, shrinking from their demise. Calvin realized he had lived his life for a few moments like this one. As Mother Nature wracked the plane, as it became more and more difficult to breath, he pulled her dress over her head and began kissing her breasts through the cups of a black lace bra. She reached down and began tugging on his manhood as though snaking a clogged drain. They groped each other clumsily, their bodies struggling to compensate for the gods' fury, to exploit the huge vibrator the plane had become. She was on top of him now, just letting him slip inside, when the bouncing and lurching and rolling and swaying and dipping slowed. Calvin felt her warm all around him, her face suddenly the beauty he'd always held at bay so it wouldn't annihilate his — not ordinary — regular life. He couldn't remember whether she'd also whispered "I love you" or if he had, as now, in the relative calm, they were becoming a spectacle. He heard nervous laughter and a few purposeful "ahems." Their bodies slowed to rest. She opened her eyes, black as all he didn't know. Suddenly he could breath again. Light as a cloud, the woman lifted herself off of him, lowered her gaze, searched the floor for her discarded dress, and returned silently to her seat.

Loins damp and mind fuddled, Calvin waited for her to touch him, say something, look his way. As she smoothed her dress, the woman's face in profile twitched as if to smile. He felt certain now. He reached out and took her hand. She let it go limp.

"I can't," she sighed, taking up her magazine, lowering her armrest, sitting silent as a shrine.

Exhausted, Calvin said nothing, watched her in silence as she read straight through to their emergency landing in Oklahoma City. When the plane reached the gate, without turning to Calvin, she said, "Excuse me," and slipped past. Again he felt a rush in his stomach, as if he were leaving for another new place. But this time the feeling left him as quickly as it had come.

Calvin stood at the baggage claim, watching the woman brush back the hair that fell naturally as night on her skin. He watched her tap the foot he'd known just an hour earlier as an instrument of bliss. She studied the conveyor belt, and, he thought, for a split second stole a glance his way. As she moved close to claim her bag, he recalled the touch of her still-young skin, and imagined himself and her as characters in a black-and-white French film. When she headed for the exit, he would forsake his luggage and hurry after her, dodging mustachioed dwarves, quarrelsome extended families, and sinister gendarmes. He would catch up with her at the exit, which would be labeled "Sortie" in gigantic gothic lettering. She would turn and simply faint into his arms. Later — And wasn't it of course ironic? — he would awaken at her flat, to find her nursing him back to health from a virus he'd caught in flight.

As she reached for her single piece of luggage, the old men and women began arriving, surrounding her, craning their loose necks to catch glimpses of pink and green ribbons tied to otherwise indistinguishable valises. Calvin watched them all, stroking hands, hugging, guiding one another tenderly away from passing dangers, sustaining themselves through their journey. Two by two they reclaimed their temporary lives and reminded each other where to find taxis. And when this gray caravan finally shuffled into the western sun, she was gone. Calvin stood for a moment beneath the departures board, then meekly walked forward to find his duffel. He stepped back to watch the unclaimed suitcases glide by, searching for a familiar shape, absorbing the absence, memorizing the scene, until an alarm sounded and the carousel clattered to a halt.

Rome

By five o'clock the battalion had mustered at 116th Street and Broadway, the main university gate. Alfie looked down the line of blue uniforms, a few, like him, in helmet and riot gear. A hundred night sticks smacked palms like the sound of upstate heat bugs, growing louder as the sun sank. If only he could be there now, at his cousin Paulie's cabin, next to his father, watching the tree line for game. Two weeks earlier the old man had gone to the emergency room, throwing up, splitting headache. Leukemia, the doctors had decided. Two months at the outside. At least he was getting to see Alfie's new son, as much as Alfie's wife would allow. He looked down the line again. The men had gone still as beagles with the beginnings of a scent. The lieutenant-in-charge was giving final instructions: They would enter through the tunnels, eject the occupiers, secure the buildings, be back at their precinct houses a couple of hours later, in bed by the time Johnny Carson was over.

The briefing room that afternoon had been all ears open, mouths shut. The brass wasn't happy about having to do this — the Department could only look bad tangling with a bunch of eggheads — but it was a detail more than a few beat cops had been looking forward to. Ever since King most of them had seen nothing but double shifts and violence from the ungrateful bastards whose neighborhoods they should've let burn. Alfie hadn't had a night at home with his kids in a week. Like a lot of his brethren, he was tired of the mulies and tired of all the unnecessary bleeding-heart shit from these spoiled brats.

"Bust their fuckin' college holes" was the way LoDato put it, lowering Monday's *Daily News*.

"Goddamn right," Alfie answered him. "A bunch of rich communists. Part of the Big Slide, LoDato. The Fall of Rome."

He'd seen a photo of Sanders, the ringleader. Typical: shaggy hair, thin, little face like a rat. Liked to hold up pictures of all the black leaders: King and the other one they killed uptown. How could his father have been that close with Joe Jefferson back upstate? Nothing but big smiles, the old preacher. And his old man trusted him, on instinct. The same old man who was always telling his sons, "Don't trust the shirt on your back." Thinking of this, Alfie had to respect Sanders at least a little, in the way he respected his dying father for stepping out of line when he needed to, the way Alfie's mother never let him do. That past weekend Sanders had gone to a faculty meeting and told the professors that unless they backed the student strike a hundred and ten per cent, everything else they did would be bullshit. The kid seemed really to believe in something, even if he was arrogant and more or less wrong. If you asked Alfie what he himself believed in, he would say maybe order, or, a bigger maybe, his family.

Truth was Alfie had become one of the cops the Department sent out to put the fear of God into the blacks. He was six-foot, three and solid muscle, from legs like a hurdler's to slim waist to weightlifter's chest and shoulders. He wore his hair military short, and had an angular, rugged, normally stubbled face that could go from wide smile to hollow stare in the second it took him to catch a whiff of trouble. His jaw was sharp as a bent elbow. His swagger was forward-leaning, promising a beating to any fool who got in his way.

Alfie leaned over to his partner Sweeney, shorter but just as solid, and grinning as if the lieutenant were up there telling stories about his latest broad.

"Their fuckin' college holes," Alfie whispered.

The smaller man's grin widened, reminding Alfie of the bastard who'd done the preacher in. Alfie always did what he had to do, but guys like Sweeney enjoyed the sound of bone on bone. Of course they were told officially hands off the students, but the warning came with a gleam in their sergeant's eye. Making an example or two usually broke up a party. If he asked, the commandants would say what his father would say: Just don't lose control. Nothing would happen until after the six o'clock news. And the reward for a job well done would be a step closer to a desk.

Alfie had done his homework and made a plan. He and Sweeney were assigned to lead the charge into Low Library. There the detail would cuff the kids and, after they went limp, what protestors usually did, drag them out onto the steps and down to paddy wagons waiting on the brick walk. The job would be all strength, like lifting a form into place on one of his grandfather's construction sites. No blows. That was the order. But Alfie knew that he and his partner and the few others in riot gear, fellas recruited from all over the city, were sent to Low for a reason. Sanders and his two goons, Lundstrem and Wiesniewski, would be there. Sanders physically was a nothing. Lundstrem and Wiesniewski were former linebackers on the Columbia football team, who'd gone over to the other side. Over the last couple of weeks, whenever a disturbance had gotten a little hairy, these two had been able to get their captain out before any shit that could have landed Sanders in the Tombs hit his fan. Today would be different. Alfie had his sights set.

"Brooklyn, Six-Eight, Seven-Three, Seven-Five, line up," the lieutenant announced.

Brooklyn. He used to feel at least a little proud of it. In the Army allegiance to the borough was their Confederate flag to wave back at the rednecks. Now even the name bothered Alfie. Most of these boys around him had grown up there, and most of them, like him, were dying to get out. His old neighborhood was still safe, but you could see it was all changing. Every day the sight of the 61st Street train ditch made him a little sicker. The chain link fence that lined the ditch was rusting away. Years ago the street had been like an estate that the whole block owned: groomed, guarded. Now people drove up in cars and dumped garbage right through the holes in the fence, or just heaved it over the top. The slope down the ditch had begun to look like an exploded landfill. Across the way the old 62nd Street guinea gardens were almost empty, most of the Italians too old to tend them. At the 65th Street station, the first ugly red graffiti had shown up a few months before. Probably the Puerto Ricans, who were taking over the far side of Borough Park, or the mulies down in Coney Island.

And the old house was no better. Even when they were kids, just moved down from Rome, it was never what you would call spacious. Since he'd been forced to marry Barbara, the situation had gotten worse and worse. Three kids now in a one-bedroom, ground-floor apartment. With his mother, who wasn't crazy about the arrangement or about his wife, living upstairs. Most of the time he hated being there, so the job came as a relief. But this last month, the outside world had become an even bigger headache. All he wanted most nights was to sit on the couch with his two older children, watch television and eat whatever piss-poor dinner Barbara put in front of him.

After eight years she was still a hell of a lot better in the bedroom, enough that he still got the kids off to sleep in time to do to her what had gotten them both here in the first place. Otherwise his wife ran around the house like a nutty partridge, flying in one direction and squawking back over her shoulder at him or at the kids, who most often were quietly doing whatever they were doing. Thank God they'd taken after *him* that way. In a house out on Long Island, Barbara might calm down, and he might have a little shop or studio, a little peace. Everything could be all right. Just to score some points with the honchos, get the detective's salary. That was the game.

His detail started their march through the black wrought iron gates, toward Low Library, between two rows of flowering cherry trees. The past-peak blossoms looked puke pink in the moonlight. Fallen petals carpeted the dark walk. Alfie remembered the story of Palm Sunday. When the troop halted, he picked up a few petals and sniffed them. They were rotten sweet. Up ahead he could see a lieutenant waving the men forward. He slipped the petals in his jacket pocket.

In the middle of campus they found themselves surrounded. Most of the crowd were students with their fists in the air and mouths open. Their shouts came in swells, like at a football game. On the lower plaza in front of the library, one group of well-dressed kids, most of them tall, good builds, tough-looking, stood inside police barricades, pointing fingers out from their pen, as though they were trying to stab the long-haired heads that stretched like a field of fuzzy weeds to every corner of the quad. Alfie nudged Sweeney. The two of them scanned the crowd of smooth-skinned faces.

A little push from the family, different timing, he could've been among them. But where? Would he have been one of the athletes in the pen? One of these Army/Navy Store or sport-coat rebels? A spectator on the lawn? More than likely he would've been sitting in his dormitory room, practicing guitar, maybe rehearsing with a band in the student lounge, maybe looking out a window every now and then. If he hadn't gone the safe route, this might've been just a big show. But then his grandfather had the business, wanted him in. And he had his music. Eddie DiMaio and their group. All his time he'd spent listening to Django Reinhardt, Doc Watson, Chuck Berry. Then there were motorcycles. And girls. And the Army.

In the end it came down to picking a uniform, holding up one sign or another. The students in the pen held up a single banner: The Majority Coalition. Most of the protestors wore buttons. Alfie walked closer to the nearest barricade, to read them: Columbia SDS, STRIKE!, "I Have a Dream", If You're Not Part of the Solution, You're Part of the Problem, IWW, Feed the Hungry! Every button screaming something so you didn't have time to think about what to think. One had a picture of two blacks wearing berets, Panthers, with the caption Political Prisoners of U. S. A. Fascism. Who were they kidding? LBJ was a prick, but he was no Mussolini. One button he saw, he liked: An old, bearded man in a fur hat, staring off in the distance, no words. A few buttons were just little red circles. These were pinned to the chests of the plainclothes people. Some plainclothes, they'd heard, had even infiltrated the occupied buildings. He pointed out the red ones to Sweeney, who nodded, grunted.

"Where's my button?" And that little smile.

Different smile but just as intense as the preacher's that morning up Delta Lake. He had to admit, Joe Jefferson had a smile that eased pain, erased worry. It was the preacher had talked his father into taking Alfie on his first hunting trip. They hadn't been an hour out when he had stopped and pointed to seven men standing on the crest of a wooded hill ahead of them. The sun still sat low behind the men, so they came at his father like dark giants.

"Bagliato!" the biggest of the bunch shouted, striding forward like a cowboy from the movies.

It was Bob Bronson, his red and black hunting cap pulled low, his round face hard to make out in the dim light. Alfie recognized the voice, and knew too well who he was and why he was there.

The man pointed to Jefferson. "Who's that you got there witcha?"

A few paces to his right, Alfie's father had stopped and was standing with his arms resting on the barrel of his upright shotgun. He spat tobacco juice in front of him.

"Friend of mine," he answered. "Business is it a yours?

In a minute the other men had surrounded their party of three. Before Alfie could move, one of them ran over, grabbed him by the arms and pulled him to the side. Instead of gunfire — He'd always known his father would never shoot a man — he heard the old man's sixteen-gauge fall in dry leaves, and turned to see his father charging at the big man's chest. Barely five-foot, eight, but solid as copper, the old man, only around forty then, hit Bronson so hard he knocked him backwards three feet.

"Sonofabitch," his father yelled, hammering punches into Bronson's face.

Then hell started raining fists. When he looked his father's way, he could see only burly arms flying up, tangles of legs and torsos, the orange, black, red, brown of the hunting clothes all the men of Rome wore this time of year. When he looked the preacher's way, he saw a different sight. One of the men Alfie knew, Lou Cinqueciocchi. He was a bartender at Bronson's bar, the Paradise, the competition for his uncle's place, the Romahawk. Lou was maybe seven, eight years older than Alfie, and had a reputation for fighting at every bar in the Italian section. This cidrul', as he'd heard his father call him, and a man Alfie didn't know were pulling the preacher's arms back around a big maple tree, tying a rope around his wrists, binding him to the trunk. Once they had him strung, Lou took out a pair of brass knuckles, pounding them into his palm, measuring his prey. Like flashlights the preacher's eyes lit up. Although he'd seen that look a few times since, for Alfie that particular flash of bloodshot white was, he understood now, prelude to the Big Slide. A split second later he heard a crack and saw actual blood as it exploded from the bridge of the preacher's nose. Then another crack. Fragments of the preacher's teeth, crushed and launched by the second blow, like sleet, peppered Alfie's jacket. A third shot, an uppercut to the jaw, put him out.

The man holding Alfie's fourteen year-old arms pushed him down to his knees.

"This whatcha wanted to see, son? Take a look. Here's what happens to niggers think they're white men."

Another roundhouse from Lou tore a hole in Jefferson's cheek. At least he was unconscious by then, Alfie recalled, marching now in single file along a narrow barricaded path, past a gauntlet of protestors. Their clothes and their songs said they didn't want violence, but their faces said something else. Snarling, like animals. They didn't know what it was to feel a club bust your gut, a gun butt smash your cheek, to bleed like you'd never stop.

Leaving most of the crowd behind, the detail jogged up a side staircase, toward Lewisohn Hall, first cutting a wide berth around the spillover, then advancing to Earl Hall, an unoccupied building that served as a social club for religious groups and that had an entrance to the system of tunnels connecting most of the buildings on campus. The one from Lewisohn to Low was the shortest, and if they were lucky, would take them right to Sanders.

Years of secret lovers' footsteps had worn depressions in the marble stairs leading down. As the tunnel lights popped on, the place began to feel almost familiar. The walls were nothing but thick concrete painted battleship gray. The whole thing looked like the basement of any big New York apartment building. It was a smell that struck Alfie peculiar. The sour smell of dirt from deep in the ground. He knew it from days playing along the Erie Canal, from excavation sites, from the Brooklyn cellar where he and his buddies had rehearsed. In those days it was mostly rock and roll, a little Elvis and Buddy Holly, what they thought people would want to hear, but always ending the night with deeper tunes, with loneliness he felt in his father's New York City exile: Hank Williams, the Stanley Brothers, Leadbelly — "Goodnight, Irene." Every time his group played it, he imagined Irene, what could have happened to her, how this singer's world could have fallen apart so fast. When they finished, he knew that everything beyond the C-D-G chords, the simple strum, was a crock of shit.

He walked on, in rhythm with the strum, Sweeney right behind him. In the distance a red light marked the entrance to Low. The protestors had thought far enough ahead to lock it, but one pick gun and the detail was in, on tiptoes now. As they crept up the first flight, Alfie made out tinny voices and music, the echoes of a family party heard from a child's bedroom. He had tried marijuana enough to know the scent, and expected to smell it any second now. It would explain the lack of a lookout at the basement door.

Drugs were everywhere. In the old neighborhood, the criminals sold them at night in front of the closed-up side-street five-and-dimes. Here, with the money these brats had, the nooks and crannies, all the deviants and rabble-rousers at the gates, the dealers probably walked the campus like they owned it. If these kids were smoking, they might be using something harder. One of them on acid might come flying down the stairs any second now. The lieutenant had told them the occupiers were unarmed, but what if they had pistols from the Black Panthers? Was he supposed to get shot so some Ivy League delinquents could make a political statement? News was the protestors had taken over the President's office, smashed the furniture, burned files, torn up the Rembrandt painting over the boss's desk. Alfie had seen a few Rembrandts and liked them. Little fucks. If anybody was going down, better them than him.

The sound from above was cover. They picked up the pace. Sweeney flew past him, two steps at a time. Alfie could hear individual guitar chords now, distorted, rough. And laughter over the music. Occasional bull-horned messages:

"You don't need a weatherman to know which way the wind blows. Yeee-hah!"

"Down with capitalism!"

"No class rank lists!"

"Fight for our brothers and sisters in the ghetto!"

"Don't trust anyone over 50!"

After each exclamation, Alfie heard a muffled cheer from the crowd on the ground.

Then one voice and line they all knew:

"Up against the wall, motherfucker!"

Alfie caught up with Sweeney and grabbed his shoulder.

"Sanders," he said, Sweeney nodding.

They flew up the stairs together like comic book superheroes, Alfie thought, their legs blue blurs, body armor heavy, nightsticks, blackjacks, walkies, and cuffs jangling against one another, sounding like castanets and wood blocks, their own music competing with the crunch of guitar chords louder and louder, the wails of solos, a black man's raspy voice. At the bottom of the last flight they surprised a kid in dungarees and polo shirt, sitting there, smoking a cigarette. He tried to turn and run up the stairs, but as Alfie got close enough to hear him wheeze, he saw the dark flash of Sweeney's billy club and heard the thud on the kid's skull. Like a scarecrow he dropped straight down, rolled a few steps to the landing below, out. Sweeney was right.

It was important to maintain the element of surprise.

Sweeney's baton rose in the air as they approached the door of the President's office. Two lines of protestors, most of them dressed for a night of drinking, locked arms across the threshold. Alfie nailed one in the belly with the butt of his nightstick, blackjacked another on the shoulder, and only had to hear the loud snap to know that Sweeney had swung right for one of their arms. That kind of pain was indescribable. A motorcycle accident had split Alfie's forearm and smashed his wrist. Out on Long Island. He had been at least an hour on the ground before the ambulance got there. A guitar solo blared from behind the door. Alfie thought about how his grandmother had later told him with the sound of the old Italian fate, "You'll never be the same." And he wasn't, not his playing, not his hope.

Sweeney's target was thrashing around on the marble floor, pawing at his shattered arm with his usable hand. You hated to hurt a dumb kid, but in a case like this you had to take out the weak link. Anyway, it was Sanders and his bunch had brought this on. Alfie wanted nothing more than to grab the asshole and personally drag him to the wagon, he hoped in front of at least two or three of the commandants. As the detail put the rest of the student guards on the ground, Alfie felt a hand on his foot. The injured kid, his face twisted like a raisin, head raised.

"Fucking hired thug," he spat between coughs.

Thug. The word his father had used after the attack in the woods. The old man lay in a hospital bed, recuperating from two broken ribs and a ruptured spleen.

"Bronson's thugs," he said. "Vigliacchi, cowards, every one of 'em. Fair fight, I'd a broken Bronson in half."

Fair fight. God bless his father. What was fair?

"He got off easy. He grabs my son, I grab an eye."

Alfie had underestimated the old man's toughness. Al Senior had gotten clear of their attackers long enough to see what Cinqueciocchi had done to the preacher. When they came at him again, his father dodged and went straight for Bronson, pinning him against a tree. He smashed the big man's head against the trunk, and while Bronson tried to push him off, Al Senior reached up and plunged two fingers into his eye socket.

"Eye's useless now. Woulda ripped it out if they hadn't a pulled me off."

The preacher wasn't so lucky. By the time the thugs fled and Alfie was able to crawl over to the big maple tree, Jefferson's face was red pulp. Only his rolling white eyes said he was still on earth. And whose fault was it? Was the old man so high and mighty he thought he could just break the rules of Rome without paying a price? Alfie was never sure he had anything to confess, and anyway it looked now like he would never get the chance.

He could feel the kid's fingers at the top of his boot. Blood surged through his legs. To stay grounded took all his strength. His chest was screaming for action, anything. His foot shook. As the kid tightened his grip, Alfie felt his teeth grind, neck burn. All around were voices shouting, so that words were twigs snapping in the woods, gunshots in the air. The kid at his feet was, what?, maybe nineteen, twenty. At that age Alfie had been a troublemaker too, always defending the neighborhood turf, trying to find a use for the muscles he'd built in his basement like a science project. His instinct now was to raise his leg and stomp the kid's hand, crush his fingers. Instead, he reached down and grabbed him by his broken arm. The kid screamed like a sick baby. Sweeney glanced over, giving him the thumbs up. Alfie threw the boy's good arm around his shoulder, and dragged him to the closest wall, and let him crumple to the ground.

"This is where you stay, you hear me?"

With a slow movement of his head, the kid signaled Alfie to come closer. Inches away from Alfie's ear, he groaned, "No matter what, we're taking the university down."

Alfie took the kid's head in both hands, slapped his cheek, and spoke slowly.

"And then what? . . . jerk-off."

The boy closed his eyes and swooned.

The battle was all about proving who had the biggest balls, and Alfie wasn't about to lose his now. Feeling another rush, he left the kid behind, more determined than ever to accomplish his mission. Butterflies in his stomach lifted him through the office door and inside. Bodies were flying all around. Some flying toward the oak-paneled walls, some flying like angry hawks at him and Sweeney. They stood back to back now, weapons up, the way his father had taught him and his little brother to do whenever wild dogs came sniffing through the woods. The other cops did the same, taking swings, connecting with the protestors who came at them in dungarees, turtle-neck sweaters, monkey dress shirts, tennis shoes. Blood streaked the floor and spattered the walls. The smell of it drove Alfie on. He stood shoulder to shoulder with Sweeney.

"Anything you see, hit."

They swung like a single four-armed monster, cracking arms, pounding backs, bashing skulls, whatever body parts had the bad luck of getting in the way. To anyone with a camera, the scene would've looked brutal, just what the bosses didn't want. But Alfie had method.

"The back," he yelled to Sweeney, "Let's go."

They were almost to the door behind the President's desk, next to the Rembrandt that somehow was still in one piece, when Alfie spotted Sanders' unmistakable head. The rebel's hair was curly, his nose straight and long — a Pinocchio nose — and he wore a green fatigue jacket. He was motioning to someone in the adjoining room, until he spotted their vanguard, Sweeney almost at the door. Turning, Sanders skipped through a thunderstorm of bodies, away.

A shoulder drove Alfie into the wall. He got to his feet. Then another shot, this one banging his head into a chair rail. He came back up swinging.

"Ahhhh, fuck."

Then Sweeney.

"C'mon, no time for that shit, Bagliato."

The room was jumping now, tilting from side to side, but Alfie clubbed his way ahead, steadying himself against the wall or a chair, or propelling himself off one of the pukes. Through the door he spotted Sweeney again, baton up, a mob whirling around him.

"Out of my way, you spoiled piece of shit."

Baton. Blackjack. Baton. Elbow. For a moment Alfie wished he'd brought brass knuckles.

The only thing brass in the room was the handle of a stand-up ashtray near a big brown leather chair. A student with a head wound sat in the chair, bleeding, holding his glasses in one hand, rubbing the bridge of his nose with the other. Above the chair Alfie saw a framed diploma, the President's: University of Wisconsin, and some Latin, . . . *scientia civilis* . . . MDCCCXXX. Numbers always looked neater that way, stronger, like counting meant something. Next to the chair was a side table with a book on it. Erasmus. *The Praise of Folly*. All of sudden Alfie felt as though he could sleep. He could sit right down here in the middle of all this shit, and read and doze off. Al Senior, a man he'd never seen read a book in his life, had told him once, as they were walking past a shelf in his Uncle Peppino's library, "Anything you wanna learn, you can find in one of these." And the world let kids like Sanders just sit in libraries and take it all in. No idea what it was to work in the dark. Sweeney should be right on his ass by now. Time to go.

The back door of the office led to another stairwell and a hallway. A few at a time, the students were finding their way down, trying to keep ahead of the riot squaders and blue coats.

"Bagliato, c'mon," Sweeney's voice called from down the hall. Alfie pushed his way through the mini-exodus. Different sets of footfalls on the marble floor echoed from around a corner. Alfie jogged the best he could toward the sound, like faint bongo drums. When he made the turn, he caught sight of Sweeney, way down, in a loping jog himself, turning around to wave him on.

Alfie's head felt full of spiders. He shook it as clear as he could, and took off running down the hall. They'd get this fuck, and that would be that.

Then Sweeney again. "Where you going, asshole?"

A group of students appeared at the next corner, running toward Alfie. They'd been holed up in another office. Did they think they were the cavalry? Sweeney was giving them all the hell he could, which slowed him enough for Alfie to catch up. As he reached Sweeney's side, they jostled with the last few students, doling out parting whacks as the dopes pushed past. Sweeney's uniform was torn at the shoulder, his face full of marks, but he was still grinning.

"He's right up there. Time he gets through the doors, we'll nail him."

Alfie followed Sweeney in a near sprint to the next stairwell. They could hear Sanders' voice, deep chipmunk, cackling, taunting.

"Up against the wall, motherfucker!"

A few seconds behind the head puke, the partners burst into the lobby. One of the goons was pushing Sanders through a side window. Alfie thought of drawing his sidearm, then thought better. Fifteen years it took him to get up the nerve to shoot a deer; it would take at least another ten for him to blast a rich kid. The goon hopped through the window, before Sweeney could catch hold of his leg. His terrier of a partner practically dove through, after their quarry. Alfie crouched down and tried not to hit his already pounding head on the sash. He emerged on the side of the library near the campus chapel, and hit the pavement running. Sweeney flashed in front of the chapel, chasing through the twilight. From one direction came a chant: "Kirk must go! Kirk must go!" The President. Sonofabitch had a living room in his office, but still, it was disrespectful. He wasn't a Hitler, this guy. Hell, he probably liked students. From another direction someone yelled, "Free Huey!" Newton, a chief Black Panther. He wouldn't mind collaring a Panther either. That would be a successful hunting trip. Good publicity. Feed the family.

By the time Alfie reached the Thinker statue, Sweeney was gone. Alfie sat down on the statue's base. Out in front of him, on the library steps, the crowd was pushing against barricades, as the protestors in the office, some hanging out the windows, called down to them.

"Pigs go home!"

"No police state."

Even the blacks treated cops with more respect.

The last straw was a banner a group of students were draping over the big statue in front of Low, the woman with open arms: "Alma Mater, Raped by Cops." Alfie turned away from the action. It was a cool night, but inside his uniform was a furnace. He took off his helmet and wiped the sweat from his forehead. In front of him rose Philosophy Hall. He looked up to see the expression on the Thinker's face. Depressed. Maybe like he didn't care or couldn't really do anything about anything. Alfie wished he had stayed in school. Up in Rome he'd loved it. Especially history, all the empires. Who was Octavian? And where did Genghis Khan come from? What made him such a bastard? They'd have stayed in Rome if it weren't for him. Or, he could say, if it weren't for his father. But was that fair? He remembered the day Johnny Bronson called him a dago, told him his father was no better than a nigger, and that's why he went around with one. He'd gone back to his father and told him.

"Why do you go around with a nigger, Pop?"

"Who's a nigger? I don't know that word." He turned to his wife. "Pen, you ever hear that word?"

Alfie's mother looked daggers at her husband, had it in for him all the time, but she just shook her head and dropped her eyes.

"Tell your friends to mind their own fathers' problems . . . and keep their minds on something other than you. Books, maybe. Girls."

But back at school Bronson and the others wouldn't let up.

"My father says your father needs to be taught a lesson, sitting with a nigger in public."

"My father says there's no such thing as a nigger."

"Maybe your father's a nigger, then."

Bronson touched Alfie's hair: curly, dark.

"You a nigger?"

Alfie shoved Bronson into a wall. They were standing outside the lunchroom, under close watch, or he would have cold-cocked the shithead.

That afternoon Alfie left school furious. On the way home, he picked up a tree branch from the woods and bashed a mailbox on the American side of town. Back at the house, he found his father underneath their old black Chevrolet.

"Pop?"

The old man groaned, sliding himself out from under the boat of a car.

"What's the story, Son?

"Kids in school today asked me was I a nigger?

His father sighed and wiped his hands on a rag.

"Why do you gotta take Joe Jefferson out in public? Can't you just be hunting friends?"

His father got to his feet, a full inch shorter than his lanky eldest.

"Alfie, I don't like to repeat myself," he said, "and I told you I don't even know what that word means. But I'll say this now and that's it . . . I love you, and I wish I could save you from the stupid people that's in the world, but, boy, sometimes you gotta pick a side and do what you know is right. Matter of fact, I'm going hunting with Joe next weekend. Up Delta Lake. And you're invited."

He patted Alfie's shoulder, and knelt down next to the sideboard of the car.

"Go tell the rascals at school if they got a problem with that, they can come out see me in the woods."

The old man disappeared under the car again.

Alfie dropped his books on the front lawn, and walked away, head down, toward Dominick Street. His life would be hell from hereon out. Johnny Bronson was always jealous of him. He wouldn't let up. And enough kids felt about blacks just the way Johnny did. Alfie hated his father sometimes. Stubborn, and then some nights he'd stay out so late, next day his mother would be nasty as a witch. Maybe his father needed a lesson. A few blocks down Alfie found himself in front of the Paradise. Inside Bob Bronson stood behind the bar, pounding the keys of the cash register. Like all Rome bars, this one had a line painted on the floor near the front. Minors could go only that far. Alfie stepped to it, ready to give Mr. Bronson all the information he had and then some.

The crackle of his walkie brought Alfie back to a chorus of 10-13s, all over the place officers in need of assistance. There were 1-4-5s, even a likely 1-8-7. Everything with the operation was going to shit. Guitar chords were blaring out here too. This time he knew the work: Jimi Hendrix. Wild, but he had a gift. When Alfie stood up, his head felt like the Thinker was sitting on it. He lurched ahead, putting into his walk all the authority he could, straightening his shoulders and clenching his fists.

At Kent Hall the music hit him like a train. Something in three-four time, crashing symbols, bass that shook the classroom windows, the switchblade guitar. He searched the walk for Sweeney. He could see here and there an NYPD uniform, but not much action. The crowd was stagnant, watching the show. Then from the direction of Hamilton Hall, over the music he heard someone yell: "Hey, Pig. Hey, white boy, whatchu lookin' for?"

Where the fuck was Sweeney?

Again, to him.

"Yo, you lose somebody, officer?"

Standing under one of the Hamilton Hall windows were two Black Panthers. The caps, the uniforms, everything but the rifles, though Alfie was sure if he frisked them he'd find pistols in their pants. He drew his revolver.

"Stay where you are, hands in the air."

The pair obliged.

After a moment of this freeze-frame, Alfie realized this was no time for an arrest — And on what grounds? He re-holstered the weapon.

The taller of the two stepped close to him and spoke.

"We was just tryin' to help you out, Brotherman."

He took another step forward, and put an arm on Alfie's shoulder.

More of his father's words: "One day a hand on the arm, the next day they're slappin' your face."

Alfie smacked the Panther's hand off. The man immediately shoved him.

"We stand our ground, Pig."

His friend drew up behind him.

"That's right. We ain't afraid o' yo' cracker ass."

Then, quick, to his side, Sweeney, tearing for the entrance of Hamilton.

His revolver again. Almost out of the holster before a hand smacked it away. The gun behind him on the ground.

Hendrix again, slicing.

Where?

The Panthers bolted.

There, by the kids with their arms in the air. Answers to every call from the pukes up front. Alfie squatted. Ankles, feet, out of the fuckin' way.

". . . KNOW WHAT I WANT, BUT I JUST DON'T KNOW . . . HOW TO GO ABOUT GETTIN' IT."

Got it. Get up. He hated this helmet, this uniform. The kids would cry if they didn't hear him come home. Even his wife would worry. Fuckin' holster. Alfie finally tucked the revolver in its bed again, took off his helmet, ran fingers through his matted, curly hair.

When he looked up, there, in his face, Wiesniewski. The stringy shag of his overgrown head. Then knuckles hissing through the air. Nose, suddenly feeling it, off-kilter, numb, wet. Falling back into another body. Thick legs coming toward him. Another shot to the temple. The pavement. Head.

Blood in his hair, on his cheek. Alfie's father lying on the ground. Dry leaves blood-stuck to his forehead. Eyes purple, swollen shut. "Joe," said his father, pointing to the tree. The sound of men yelling, car doors slamming, an engine, a screech of wheels. Sirens: cruisers, wagons, fire trucks. A herd's worth of footsteps, one ear, the other. His father pushing him off a path when the cows came through. Pop in the leaves, blood, ooze on his sleeve, arm extended. "Joe." Sky, pink. Cuffs, denim. Sandals. Gravel. Stink of dirt, feet. Roll. Roll over, cover up.

". . . MAKE LOVE, YOU BREAK LOVE, IT'S ALL THE SAME . . . WHEN IT'S OH-VAH."

A boot in his ribs. Motherfucker. Not dying here, for this. The baton. Fence. Take a hold. Half-punch on his neck. Up. Shouldn't a missed, punk. Baton. Swing.

Wiesniewski, staggering. Around him too many kids, like this was some outdoor dance, shoulders bouncing up and down. Red lights flashing. Riot squad on its way. Their whistles. Wiesniewski, back at him.

"Up against the wall, pig."

"Only wall I see is right behind you, asshole."

Alfie swung the club with all he had into the ex-jock's side. He groaned, doubled over. The only cop in the Bagliato family brought the baton down again, double-fisted, on the middle of the kid's back, heard the breath leave him. Wiesniewski tried to turn and run, still bent, stumbling, half-sideways, another berserk dance. What difference did it make? The whole world was going berserk. Alfie slammed another shot into the back of his right knee, and Wiesniewski went down against the side of Hamilton. Would've happened to him anyway. Some game nobody'd remember, and he'd be a gimp for life. At least he could tell his grandchildren it was for a cause. The kid got to his feet, a painful, slow climb, leaned back against the wall, looking up. Staring at the sky, a baby. Then, like fire, he leapt at Alfie, a roundhouse blocked with the baton.

"Ahhh."

A return straight right to the kid's chops, blood from his mouth as he slumped again against the wall, like a beaten boxer.

How much can you take?

"Joe," his father had moaned, "Cut him down."

Alfie shuffled over to the big maple. The preacher's face was ruined, but the real horror was his body, curved and bent almost at ninety degrees to his hips, ankle snapped under one leg. Alfie got out his pocketknife and sawed at the ropes until first one arm, then the other came free and shot forward. Jefferson fell to the ground with a cry you could barely hear even in the quiet of the woods. Alfie dragged him out in time to save his life, his father able only to help move the preacher's limbs into some kind of proper place for the haul. He was weeks in the hospital before a relative, a brother or cousin, came to take him away, for good.

A few hours later Alfie was back at the house, shaken, a few cuts on him, but okay, curled under his mother's protective wing. Sitting there, patting her boy's head, she must have seemed to the old man the picture of satisfaction, like she'd won a battle.

"Soon as your father's out of the hospital," she told Alfie, "we leave for Brooklyn. Grandma and Grandpa have the rooms all made up. Your father will meet us there."

Brooklyn. New York City. Everything and nothing. Here was this kid, probably some businessman's or shop-owner's son, crippled and on his way to jail, and for what? Was he freeing the blacks? Was he stopping the war? Alfie understood now what his father knew, why he spent so much time in bars, or out hunting, always changing jobs. Nobody was free. Whoever built these buildings would still run things. You could work for them or against them. You could stay in the city or you could leave. Where were you gonna find peace? Wiesniewski would have kids, and then he'd be right next to Alfie, maybe with a little bigger house, in a neighborhood or town with not so many skells. Maybe the only difference was how far you traveled to reach the woods.

He grabbed Wiesniewski's arms and twisted them around his back, snapped on the cuffs. The kids around them noticed, and turned on Alfie.

"Fascists!"

"Police brutality!"

"Cop thugs, go home!"

Where the fuck was Sweeney?

Suddenly water was dripping on Alfie's head. He pulled Wiesniewski a step away from the wall and looked up. He spotted Sanders and Lundstrem leaning out of a second-story window, mid-spit. Down the building a little ways, in the next window, he spotted Sweeney.

"Can't get at 'em down there. Door's blocked," his partner yelled. "You all right?"

He raised an open palm, to say everything was under control.

In the meantime, Alfie saw Lundstrem climbing out on the ledge. The mob below cheered as he got to his feet.

"Your baton" Sweeney called, pointing to a spot in front of where Alfie stood, "you're gonna need it."

Carefully, carefully, Alfie moved forward again. One hand still on Wiesniewski, he bent over to pick the weapon up.

"Yeeee-haaah!" someone yelled, the sound Dopplering.

Then he felt the weight of a hundred trees fall on his back, his legs shoot out from under him, his face slam against the concrete. For a minute, black swirls and distant chords behind his eyelids, then red, then almost light, then a body next to his: Lundstrem, his limbs dancing in pain, hands grabbing at the bone protruding from his leg. Alfie tried reaching for him, but couldn't move. Not an arm, not a muscle.

All around was chaos. A swarm of blue uniforms yanked students from the scene, clubbing the ones who didn't move fast enough. They formed a circle around Alfie and the kamikaze. One of the cops lay down on the ground, looking him in the eye.

"Don't try to move. Ambulance is almost here."

The old man's first day in the hospital was like this, the i. v. fresh in his veins.

"They want you to stay still, Pop, get your strength back."

His father nodded pathetically. At sixty, he was still a specimen, arm all muscle around the needle and tube. Some days he lay there like stone. Some days you'd never know he was dying. Every day they talked: about work, about the baby, about his mother, the weather, football, but never about Rome.

The prone cop tried consoling Alfie.

"The boys are breaking down the door right now. Gonna ream those pieces of shit a new one. And don't worry, this collar has your name on it."

Alfie blinked, then closed his eyes, listening to the strange quiet, the shouting and fighting fading far away as the horizon. Even the cops had gone quiet, standing vigil. Minutes. He remembered the petals in his pocket, spring on the block or back in Rome, then tried to picture his kids. Their features escaped him, lost as the preacher's. The best he could do was imagine a house with faceless children standing in front of it, waving, and then himself, at a distance he couldn't cover, sighting them through the old binoculars his father used for the hunt.

ANGEL BOY

Millie, always with the eye, peered into the carriage, smiled at Ida and Dottie, and said, "He's too beautiful. You're gonna lose him."

The baby giggled, and Dottie, sweet Dottie, reached into the carriage and lifted the swaddled boy to her shoulder, holding him in front of her like a communion wafer, like the Baby Jesus she kissed every morning, praying for a son of her own. Poor Dottie, who no matter how much noise she made in the other bedroom couldn't make a baby with Ida's brother. This was three years now. Ida stayed home, praying for her sister-in-law. Brooklyn was supposed to be the borough of churches, so something should happen.

Two weeks later Ida's baby boy was dead. In his crib, beautiful mouth and eyes open wide. Doctor Paglia couldn't say why he was gone. The most beautiful baby boy. One of those blond-haired, blue-eyed Italian babies from paintings. So beautiful, Ida thought, that pictures of him never came out. Dottie had always taken the film to be developed. But either the sun had been too bright or her husband had exposed the film or maybe whoever developed the pictures had kept the ones of Little Frankie for himself, to show his wife how beautiful their baby could be.

"When the sunlight hit his curls," Dottie told Ida and the others at the funeral, "he looked like one of the angels." Dottie led them, all the women of the neighborhood, in making the sign of the cross. Dottie might have been an idiot, but Ida could see in her face that it was like she had lost her own. Millie came over to hug her. Ida stood there, like Dottie, unable now to cry, watching and listening as though she were floating above the room. She watched Millie's lips.

"I know you loved him," she heard Millie say. "We all did."

All their faces said the same, and no one cried.

"Like one of the angels," Ida whispered that night to her sleeping husband, her tears blurring the shadowy ceiling where every night blue and red neon flashes from the street shops made patterns Ida thought she could read, especially when all was quiet, when Dottie and Dominick weren't done doing what they did, which she and Francesco hadn't done since she had told

Francesco she was expecting, and Dottie had told them they would have the most beautiful baby on earth.

Too beautiful. The hair, but more the eyes, like little blue flames, so beautiful that women who saw him stared at him like they were under a lover's spell, in love and a little afraid. Dottie told Ida that from the first and only time Ida brought the baby to the beauty parlor the women never stopped talking about how beautiful he was: his perfectly round face, his perfect little hands, his smile that never ended, each of his eyelashes like a whisper from God. Like a little girl, Dottie repeated it to Ida just the way they'd said it. They even asked Dottie for a picture for the big mirror. Everybody would want to come in and see him. The women also said he was cursed. Since Dottie was an idiot, they weren't afraid to say it in front of her. Ida could see them in the beauty parlor, with their coffee, with their hair in curlers.

"You always knew she wouldn't have a normal baby." said one. "You remember how her mother talked."

"He came straight from heaven to her, and had to go back. That's all," said another.

"She always got what she wanted, and that's a curse," said the first woman, with satisfaction.

"Some things," said a third, "we're not supposed to have."

But Ida didn't believe in curses. Even if she did, she was always too busy with something to do — to cook or clean or change diapers — to worry about them.

When she thought of it now, it seemed to Ida that from the time he was born she had been too preoccupied with chores to see her Frankie's beautiful face or hear his voice and say what a mother should say to her baby. But thank God for poor, sweet Dottie, how she watched the beautiful boy when Ida wasn't there or was too tired to sit and adore him.

As beautiful as the angels he was, and when Dottie was getting dressed for Mass, Ida in her housecoat, from the top step of the brick stoop, could swear she heard him leading the Sunday morning choir. That first beautiful note, nothing special as far as being too high or too low, but just the right length for his little angel voice to carry. "Aaaahhhh . . ."

"Ave Maria," Ida sang under her breath, knowing that even though he'd been dead only a few weeks, her baby Frankie boy was an angel who knew much more than she did. She began to cry as Frankie led the choir through the final refrain. "Ave Maria," she mouthed. "Ave Maria. Be good to my boy."

As his perfect voice glided to the "i" in "Maria," Ida could see his little wings beat faster and faster, lifting him to the frescoed ceiling above the choir and out over the faithful in their pews, until he drew all heads upward, all eyes from the altar to his rosy cheeks, to his curls lit by streams of sunlight through the blue stained glass, to his little blue flame eyes lighting and warming the whole congregation.

Ready for Mass, Dottie all in black stepped through the front door and sat next to Ida. Ida took Dottie's hand and got to her feet. She kissed Dottie's forehead, pulled Dottie to her, like a child.

"He's an angel, Dottie. You remember how round his little face used to be? With those blue eyes. How he used to laugh when anybody looked in the carriage. It was like he knew how beautiful he was."

"He belongs to everybody now," Dottie said, leaving Ida to the echo of church bells chiming the next hymn.

Every Sunday morning, even the day they baptized Dottie's own little boy, years after Little Frankie joined the angels, instead of going to Mass with Dottie, Ida sat on the stoop and listened to him sing the "Ave Maria." The years passed this way, with Ida liking Sundays less and less. When the "Ave Maria" ended, the day was over. Where before she would tease Dottie and Dominick about their bedroom serenades, about their wish to have as many babies as the church had saints, or she would kick her husband under the table for forgetting his pleases and thank yous for a passed bowl of *scarol'*, now she dreamt standing up, sitting down, serving, of the little angel boy her mother had told everyone in the family and the neighborhood that Ida would someday have because Ida had been born with light hair, and because she had found the perfect man, the most handsome, blue-eyed Italian boy in Brooklyn, whose uncle was a bishop in the old country. Ida had always believed this, because she believed in blessings. In Italy Ida's mother had lost three children, all boys, and the Blessed Virgin owed her daughter this.

So when her mother was alive Ida did what every other daughter in the neighborhood did: helped clean and cook, walked to the greengrocer's for the *scarol'*, to the *latticini* for the *muzzarell'*, to the paneficio for fresh semolina bread, everyday, like the other girls, making jokes with them, which always ended with punchlines about men, marriage and babies, while Ida's head was full of her mother's prediction, her knowledge of a perfect baby boy. Ida could sense everyone knew, so she told the whole family, all her friends, Dottie and Millie, and they believed every word. Millie wanted to know everything. Dottie knew nothing. "Day and Night," Ida called them. Nothing in common, except they both wanted babies worse than anything in the world, and they both had the eye, always stopping on the street to look into carriages and coo at the ones with the chubbiest cheeks and shiniest curls.

Millie, God rest her soul, died during Mass one Sunday, of a hemorrhage, they said, while the choir was singing the hymn over the Eucharist, not too long after Little Frankie. It was the most beautiful death Dottie had ever seen and Ida could ever imagine. While the choir was singing the cadenza, "He is joy for all ages," Millie, who was sitting in Dottie's pew, looked up, spread out her arms, and fell backward, her dead weight balancing on the polished walnut benchback, like a warped see-saw, her mouth and eyes open to heaven.

"If only they were playing the 'Ave Maria,' it would have been even more beautiful," said Dottie, her face placid and getting, it seemed, more perfect with age. Sweet, stunad' Dottie, who no matter what happened, even when Ida's little angel left them, never cried or laughed for more than a second. As the years passed, the only crying Ida ever heard from Dottie, come to think of it, was at night when Ida could hear her sobbing — it had to be — for her dead husband, Ida's brother Dominick, who had died in Dottie's bed during their last serenade, afterwards Dottie knocking on her door, stone-faced, walking like a ghost to Ida's window, Francesco still sleeping, and Dottie staring out, the street lights turning her face red and blue.

Most nights now Ida could hear Dottie working up to it, sniffling, choking up, then letting go with big boo-hoo sobs like in the pictures. Then a few sobs that sounded like grunts. And then Dottie would be asleep, probably dreaming of Jesus, she was so good, the poor thing.

After Dominick passed away, may he rest in peace, Ida babysat Dottie's baby, the harelip, poor *disgraziat'*. Cute in his way, but even after the operation, Ida could see he would never be right. Like his mother, he watched

Ida's eyes, but he wasn't all there. Still, Ida loved him. He was part of the family. He was Dottie's joy and her cross. He belonged to all of them.

Eventually, Ida even stopped going to the beauty parlor. Her husband didn't look at her, and without a baby carriage to push around the neighborhood, what was the use? But whenever Dottie came back from getting her hair done, she would tell Ida how, even after years, they all talked about Frankie and the curls and cheeks and eyes and lashes they still wished they had a picture of. One of the women had even done a pencil sketch of Little Frankie from memory and put it up on the big mirror. Dottie said she told her the eyes weren't big enough and the curls weren't as curly as Frankie's, but it was the best they could do for the most beautiful baby any of them had ever seen. And underneath the picture someone had written on the mirror, in lipstick, "Our Boy."

From when he was a baby the harelip stayed with Ida on the stoop while Dottie went to church. Ida watched his face, waiting for his stupid expression to change. And she rocked him while she and Frankie sang the "Ave Maria." He grew older, and still she saw nothing in his face. When he was almost four years old, he spoke his first word, if Ida could call it that. It sounded just like the first note of the beautiful hymn, the "Aaahh. . . ," but not steady and beautiful the way her own little angel could make it sound.

One Sunday, when the harelip was five years old, he came down with a virus. Ida, as usual, sat on the stoop, watching families pass by, while Dottie, as usual, sat in church, her head bowed. A few minutes before Frankie would sing the "Ave Maria," Ida felt a little hand on her shoulder, waking her from a daydream of her little boy. She shivered.

"Johnny," she sighed, smoothing the harelip's bangs. He took Ida's hand and pulled her into the house, up the stairs, his straight black hair swaying from side to side as he led her, like a little dog with the scent of an animal, pulling her with all his might until they reached Dottie's room. Ida looked in. On the dressing chair near the bed — strange thing — Dottie had laid a pair of her dead husband's underpants.

Dottie's sobbing and grunting and — it seemed like words — her talking too had been especially loud the last few nights, so that they sounded like conversations through the wall. Dottie was talking to her dead husband, so much like a little boy himself when he was alive, God bless him. Dottie had laid out his clothes to remember him, to take care of him like she'd always done, like Ida had done before Dottie. That was it. God bless them all, the poor things.

Johnny tugged at Ida's hand again, pulling her to Dottie's closet, deep, neatly arranged — She was the neatest idiot Ida had ever seen. Inside the closet, Ida switched on the light. Dresses hung in the middle, a couple of feet off the ground, surrounded on either side by men's suits, Dominick's, and on the floor, neatly stacked, boxes of shoes. The arrangement left enough room for the harelip to walk under the dresses. He pulled Ida in after him and headed for the back wall. She had to part the row of dresses and crouch low to follow. Ida straightened up and looked around at the clothes. Dresses and suits that looked familiar, and ones she could swear she'd never seen before, everywhere a new color.

That's why he'd brought her here. He loved to sit, like his mother, and stare at beautiful things, to touch them, mute. Maybe he'd found his way in here early this morning, sat for an hour while Dottie dressed, though Dottie had said to keep him out of her room when she wasn't home, which Ida, until now, always did. His first day alone in Mommie's room, and the harelip went for the closet. *Stunad'*. He had sat here this morning, staring at the colors, and made his sounds like the "Ave Maria." Lost in the thought and a vision of her own child, Ida barely noticed Johnny tugging at her skirt. Little bastard, though she loved him, born later the same year her brother died, so sweet, like Dottie, so dependent, like Dominick, Ida's Sunday companion but never her own little angel boy.

Ida looked down to see the harelip pointing a tiny finger at the back wall, at something hanging there like a string, hanging from a big nail. She bent down to get a better look. This close to the floor, the light from the dusty bulb didn't help much. Ida squinted but still couldn't see what it was. The harelip reached out and rubbed it between his fingers. As he did, Ida, down on her knees, her eyes coming level with the nail, could begin to make it out, bright as the sun, a lock of hair, curly, wound twice around the nail, one end of it driven into the plaster. Golden hair, and next to it a picture — *Madonna Mi'!!* — a picture of her little Frankie in his carriage, smiling his beautiful smile, his little cherub arms raised up, reaching out. Ida had taken the picture herself, and given it up, like all the others, for lost.

The harelip started to giggle, then squeal like a little baby, pushing Ida over, so that she fell against something hard and cold. She lifted herself up and saw it was the reel-to-reel tape recorder, Dottie's tape recorder from years ago, plugged into an extension cord that led back into the bedroom. Ida switched it on and heard a buzzy hum like the sound of an empty house she knew so well, the sound of a child, maybe the harelip, sleeping. Then a sound that hit her like a lightning bolt from God Almighty. Her little angel boy's voice, her little Frankie, the "Aaaahhhs" he sent out to all his worshippers, the girls at the beauty parlor who adored him, people on the street who caught his eye in the carriage, the family, anyone who had ever laid eyes on her beautiful boy. Ida slumped against the wall, sat with her mouth open, her eyes fixed on the harelip swaddled in the colors of Dottie's wardrobe.

That night Ida lay thinking about the years she had put up with this: her husband still out while she lay in bed, waiting for sleep, watching the lights play on the ceiling and hearing her beautiful angel's voice singing the "Ave Maria," and the lights changing pattern with every note. He sang tonight, and as Ida listened she thought of the shrine the harelip had shown her, and she began to sob like poor Dottie: for her husband who was out with another woman or maybe a bunch of other women — Who could know? — for Dominick, who never knew his own son; for Johnny, who would never know the things an angel knew; for her own little angel beautiful boy.

Ida sobbed a sob that shook her until she felt cold and wet from tears. Then she heard Dottie sobbing too. But Dottie was with her son, not alone tonight. Was he sick? God forbid. What would poor Dottie do without him? Look how much she had wanted a son, that she stole pictures and built a shrine. Ida could forgive her for that. Johnny was a cross, after all, and they were both idiots, the two of them, but they were all each other had, Dottie and her harelip boy, *poveracc'*. Ida dried her cheeks, put on her robe and slippers, and went to check on them.

Ida stood with her hand on Dottie's doorknob, a little mad at Dottie now, when she thought about it, mad for keeping a secret about her angel boy, but sad too, for everyone. Ida's mother had promised her the most beautiful boy, which she had had, but since then nothing but memories of him and her mother and her brother Dominick and Ida's own bastard of a husband Francesco who wasn't even there to say nothing and eat, who would probably be out fooling around with her *puttann'* of a friend Millie right now if she hadn't died so beautifully during the Holy Mass.

Dottie cried louder as Ida turned the knob, as she opened the door. Was Johnny that bad off? God love him. Why didn't Dottie just ask for her help? Sweet, *stunad'* Dottie, poor, sweet Dottie, poor soul, the poor thing, until the moment Ida saw them there: Dottie and Francesco, Ida's Francesco, on the bed, him between her legs, and the harelip in the closet doorway, and Dottie's face turned toward the door, tears running down her cheek, her eyes meeting Ida's not so much with surprise, Ida thought, but with sympathy.

"Isn't he beautiful, Ida?" Dottie wept. "Our beautiful boy."

Ida gasped loud enough for everyone to hear, but before Francesco had time to take his rotten thing out of poor Dottie, Ida had run back to her room and locked the door. Through the wall she could hear Francesco cursing. "*Puttana Diavolo!*" she could make out, and the slamming shut of Dottie's door, then pounding on hers. Francesco pounded and pounded for almost an hour, but Ida wedged a chair under the doorknob and lay on the bed, flat on her back, like death, until her bastard of a husband gave up and went to sleep on the couch or maybe — Who could put it past him now? — back to poor Dottie.

Ida remembered as she lay, the look on the harelip's face, his eyes on fire and his mouth like the circle mouth of a choir angel hitting notes only God could hear. And when everything was quiet finally, she heard little footsteps in the hallway. The little harelip angel was going downstairs. She could follow him. It was safe. Francesco had to be asleep by now. Ida slipped into her housecoat, stepped into her slippers, and tiptoed down the stairs.

So many times on Sundays, those times Dottie was away praying for all the souls, Ida had carried Dottie's poor boy in her arms, like her own. Dottie was praying for her Frankie, so the least she could do was hold the little *disgraziat'* in her arms, walk him so he could hear her own little angel sing, so he could know for a while what the cherubs knew. Ida loved him now.

When she found Johnny on the couch, she took him, half-asleep and heavy — getting to be a real boy — in her arms. He clung in his sleep, like a beautiful baby, and she walked. His black hair between her fingers. The moon. The poor harelip, the little angel, moaning, "Aaaahh. . . ." Ida remembered how the monsignor made a point of never locking the church doors. Ida walked into the street and the crisp night air, around the corner to the church, up the marble steps cold through her slippers. Johnny was beginning to open his eyes. She took the steps as fast as she could. Years she hadn't been inside. She pulled open the heavy door with one arm and all the strength her little angel had left her.

Some days Ida wasn't sure how she'd even leave the house to get the bread. Dottie had done her a favor. Poor, sweet Dottie. Ida could see her now kneeling down in the back of her closet, stroking the lock of their beautiful angel boy's golden hair.

A big moon lit the stained glass Stations of the Cross. The harelip's hair and dark eyes glowed golden as Ida carried him up a side aisle to the baptismal font, where she rested him and poured water over his forehead. She'd been dreaming for years of her Frankie in this church, but now it was like a place she'd never seen before, like the back of Dottie's closet.

Poor Dottie was sitting in front of the reel-to-reel now. She flipped the switch. Her angel's voice. The colors of suits and dresses she never wore like moonlit clouds in the darkness. Moonlight lit the church altar pale blue. If Ida could paint, she'd paint this scene, and they'd put the picture in a museum and tell her she was inspired by God.

Sweet Dottie was listening to the recording of their boy when it began to sing.

"Aaaaahhhhhh-vaaaaaayyy-Maaaahhh-reeeee-eeee-eee-aaaahh!"

Ida could hear it too as she brushed strands of wet hair from the harelip's open eyes, and he smiled at her, as Dottie, with Frankie's voice filling the house, came downstairs to get her boy, who kept smiling under water, as Ida held him there, held his beautiful face, so round and almost perfect, too beautiful in the pale light to look at, and hearing her angel sing again, held the final note in a whisper.

THE NEW POPE

Yes, I know they shot Sister Leonella, but what can I do? There is no real absolution for the Pope. Of course I feel terrible, as terrible as one can feel for a nun one has never met. Well, if I did receive her, I don't recall now. Do you have any idea how many nuns a Pope encounters in a single day? Enough surely to fill the Raffaele Rooms, I can tell you that. Yes, yes, I love them too. The colors. Ah, but they nuns can be too much. I see you understand.

This Leonella, they shot her in Somalia. Fortunately, I'm not scheduled to visit there. Where? Turkey? Can we call and tell them some other time? Madonna, have mercy. They should realize I was only quoting, and it was only a lecture to theology students. They weren't even paying close attention. One in the back was snoring. Can you imagine, snoring at the Chief Ambassador of Christ? The "Prophet of Evil" comment at least got a response. But, ah, no more will I take suggestions for material from Cardinal LaPoint. Not that he is an entirely foolish man. I agree with him that we have much to learn from the fourteenth century. I can assure you, if the institution of matrimony were now what it was in those days, the laity would need the Holy Church more than ever. We could resume the practice of distributing food and medicine to families after Mass. Local administration has always been our forte. Success at that level could even spell a return to tithing. I believe, in fact, that under my predecessor, bless his name, we experimented with this formula in Africa and the South Pacific. More and more there we compete with the Muslims. I'm loath to admit it, but they appear to be winning that battle. To some extent, yes, it's a result of low overhead. They'll work from a storefront, a café, a cave, even telecommute. Indeed, my boy, let us not forget to summon the Webmaster and schedule e-platform training sessions for all visiting bishops. Ah, will we ever regain the upper hand? Perhaps silent détente is best.

Perhaps we should have begun our recent talk with passages about poverty and disease. Still, the point was only to suggest, subtly, just the opposite of what my words appeared to say. I should also have mentioned the joy, peace and beneficence we rightly ascribe to Christ, but I felt this would be a bit patronizing. So often the Muslims lack a sense of humor in matters of faith. Can you imagine their ban of pictorial representation? No holy men in the desert, no celestial virgins. Think of the paintings they could have produced, the museums, the revenue! And now they cry poverty. It's enough to make a monk's cat laugh. They don't scruple when I appeal — and you know as well as I that here lay my true motive — when I appeal for, and I quote myself, "for a clear and radical refusal of religion as a motivation for violence." Those words, our first official apology, flowed from my own pen. But did the Muslims heed them? No, instead their people constructed a very life-like effigy of the Pope, and not only burned it, but then doused the flames and quartered the iconic remains. It's true, my son, that the voice of hypocrisy sings loudest in the light of day.

Much as they comfort, words may also deceive. The price we pay is a junket to Turkey. And then where? Indonesia. Why, it's as if I were begging Our Gracious Lord to have me assassinated. Naturally, we'll send a decoy in advance, an actor without family. It's a tedious journey, so we must offer him well above clerical impersonation scale. Money well spent, for your sake and mine. Remember that any beheading of us is a double decapitation: the king without a head, the land without a king, and all that. A pity we cannot claim Shakespeare for our own.

Whatever the case, this apology tour may be the opportunity to convey our message to the masses living in the Muslim sphere of influence. If A. C. Milan can win on the road, so can we. When I say that these words about the great Mohammed do not reflect my personal views, you may be certain, my young friend, that I will eagerly expand on those views: to wit, the love for all that is Christ, whose earthly representative, of course, yours truly and in everlasting peace happens to be. For now, however, it appears that my well-phrased "*Sono ramaricato*" is less than sufficient. Must I be so literal as to say "*mi dispiace*"? "I regret." "I'm sorry." What difference could there be? On top of multiple exculpations, the Muslims must also, apparently, dictate my Italian diction.

And why does the press insist on printing the most provocative passages from the speech *del giorno*? They may shoulder their share of the blame. This Muslim Brotherhood is a self-anointed cabal of fanatics who pontificate about the belief and practice of a religion that rightfully belongs to God, but they too read the papers. What are you staring at? Hand me my slippers.

Ah, Guglielmo, globalization is proving itself, at best, a mixed blessing. It must have been lovely in the fourteenth century, to issue decrees from the Holy See without contrition or fear of reprisal. Or were those the Schism years? Forgive me. At my age names and dates lie on a distant horizon. But as I was saying, it must have been a pleasure for past Popes to issue decrees and then simply wait for dignitaries to respond to nuncios, to sojourn to the Vatican, to implore, to negotiate, to pledge allegiance. Today, the Pope is reduced to traveling like a performer, like the blessed Pavarotti in his prime. Dead at seventy, a youngster by our standards. Must I really visit Malaysia? Indonesia, yes, of course. But is it absolutely necessary? Then, I think, well, certainly it is. Those people also have souls, and those souls yearn for direction, and the visits are, after all, televised.

Our goal then must be absolute security and comfort. We must guard against the human frailty we'll be declaring epidemic. Travel by ship would be best of all: better meals, midnight strolls along the aft deck, a well appointed martini bar. But this new public would never stand for the appearance of leisure in our evangelism. If we make ecumenical noises, we must reach the bar the Protestants have set. They bring the energy of terriers to their work. Alas, we shall fly. We may of course summon LoSpuntino, the pastry chef, to our side, though Caponuzzo, the saucier, claims he has commitments that preclude travel. His mint-laden lamb shanks are an incalculable loss. You and I and a small staff aboard the Vatican jet. Have we arranged for in-flight films? And what of the lavatory? Few enough are the pleasures of an airborne pontiff. If they ask, I prefer Westerns, although a good romantic comedy always warms the heart. Who? No, I'm not familiar with her work. What else has she appeared in? Yes, a few Hollywood magazines would indeed enlighten me.

Tell me, do I worry over nothing? Am I not on record as a healer? Have I not often pleaded for interfaith tolerance and cooperation in productive intolerance? Yes, warm milk would be lovely, but with, if you please, just a whiff of brandy. But I was speaking of cooperation. "The dialogue," I said, "cannot be reduced to an optional extra." I love the casual redundancy of "optional extra." It has a nearly physical force. I smile whenever I see it in print. Then too I was speaking on the relationship between faith and reason, belief and knowledge, religion, if you like, and science. The emperor whose words I borrowed was surely displaying his ignorance of other religions as well as his ignorance of the power of belief, when he categorized the one they like to call "The Prophet" as evil. I've always thought it odd that the supreme figure of their faith, the one to whom they devote their entire being, was merely a prophet. Any world needs a savior, isn't that so? Prophets don't, per se, save. Jeremiah, for example. A great prophet, one of the top five, but whom did he save? Bereft of the savior trope, the people of God would immediately blow themselves to Kingdom Come. Of course I know that's what's happening already, but, you see, these are the wages of placing a mere prophet on the highest pedestal. What about Oklahoma City? My boy, it only serves to prove my point. A Christian has a savior, a clear path to salvation. He therefore will not annihilate himself, which, in any case, our Holy Scripture prohibits, although, yes, on occasion, he will, if he feels righteously compelled, blow others to smithereens. This discourse may in fact be the subject of my first interfaith proclamation. We don't? Why not? Is our audience not all the people of God? Remember, souls are our business.

As you well know, I've never been afraid to ruffle feathers. How would it strike you, then, the issuance of an edict, or even a bull, decreeing — Perhaps "decreeing" is a bit strong — recommending . . . all right, suggesting that all the souls of the world appeal to religious leaders, no matter how Godforsaken their faith, for a savior to which they might swear undying devotion as model of, mind you, piety and peace? Naturally, we would cloak the suggestion in the finery of a wider-ranging decree about hope, the eradication of hunger, and the equal validity of all cultures' customs and cuisines. Would I seem too bald-faced in my intent? You know I mean well. I only want what the Lord tells me is best for everyone.

Yes, what of the treatment of women? Is the time right for me to kick that hornet's nest again? So long as their men stop short of the two M's, murder and mutilation, women of the Arab world will manage, won't they? Are you certain? But doubtless their ululations are enough to fend off even the most determined abusive husbands or fathers. Ah, now look here! The velveteen underside of my robe is worn. Do you want my naked buttock rubbing against this course upholstery? It's 400 years old if it's a single day. These are our traditions and cares. Patrimony, lad. Take heed. There. Now, we were speaking of mutilation. There is? A lot? And murder? Isolated cases, to be sure. I'm not certain most national leaders could even locate Oman on a map. And then they might point fingers back at us, with all this Opus Dei rigamarole. God grant these Hollywood producers their wizardry, but sometimes I do loathe them. How could any son of the Church, much less the son of God, find pleasure and comfort in a woman? It defies clerical logic. Save for the seldom monastic tryst or appeal to the Blessed Mother. Even the Muslims must admit that Mariology is a winning big idea. I once heard an Italian Muslim yell *"Madonna Mi'!"* as if the Immaculata were standing next to him, which, of course, she was.

What we need most in this time of crisis is a good synod. We haven't had one in two generations, and then it was all about the Jews. You weren't even a gleam in your father's wandering eye, but he can tell you, I'm sure, of the excitement in the air, even among the lowest of the lowly laity. We were undoing seven centuries of doctrinal drift and clumsy semantics. With mighty strokes of pens, the Holy Fathers banished from our realm the sacred cow of conversion. If the Crusades couldn't do it, if the Jews wouldn't give in to Hitler, how could we carry on with our presumption? At the time, in fact, the Church was experiencing something of a lull, a humble period, as you may recall from your reading. Vatican II lifted our spirits, gave us reason to be proud. No longer would the ignorant revere Simon of Trent; no more would we abide by the injunctions of the First Lateran Council. Yes, Anno Domini 1215, very good. I hope the brothers rewarded you with a fine grade in that course. Yes, it was the whole business of watching that Jews didn't exact too high an interest from Christian debtors. Mind you, given the rise of Jewish defense organizations and Holocaust remembrance societies in those days, the Church could easily have assumed a defensive posture against the spiritual interest Jews were then seeking to collect. Why do you frown? I am only voicing the thoughts that used to trouble me. Our own collective guilt for their collective guilt — yes, as in the vulgar expression, *"'Mazza Crist'"* — threatened to overwhelm us. Thanks to Our Lord and Savior, our collective grace prevailed, and we chose to stand upon pillars of our best faith, such as Pius V, who announced to the world that the Jews never would knowingly have crucified the Lord of Glory. 1566? May the good brother, your preceptor, God grant him favor, forever carry such dates in his ironclad mind.

God willing, we can meet the Muslims soon on neutral ground, somewhere safe, protected but sufficiently Arabic in character to satisfy them. Sicily! My boy, let no one say you lack for diplomatic acumen or cultural sensitivity. Sicily, yes, Palermo *se stessa*, the outskirts, some fine Moorish palace by the sea. White glove service of hors d'oeuvre. How I love the rice balls. They come also without meat, that our Muslim brethren may partake. In good humor they may even agree to reclassify all Muslims. Then they may have Mecca officially condemn one or two rogue groups. In return we might easily condemn some or another Christian phalange. Both this strategy and the menu require further contemplation.

For now I would have you fluff my pillows and pray with me for a bountiful harvest from the apostolic seeds we are plotting to plant in . . . Indonesia, Borneo is it? . . . in those far-off lands as well as in our beloved Sicily. Here is the kernel of colloquium, of fellowship with the Turk, of a third great council yielding the sort of revised doctrine that even a Muslim publisher would be tempted to circulate in trade.

VIA FOLIOS
A refereed book series dedicated to the culture of Italians and Italian Americans.

ROBERT VISCUSI, *Ellis Island*, Vol. 74. Poetry. $30

ELENA GIANINI BELOTTI, *The Bitter Taste of Strangers Bread*, Vol. 73, Fiction, $24

PINO APRILE, *Terroni*, Vol. 72, Italian American Studies, $20

EMANUEL DI PASQUALE, *Harvest*, Vol. 71, Poetry, $10

ROBERT ZWEIG, *Return to Naples*, Vol. 70, Memoir, $16

AIROS & CAPPELLI, *Guido*, Vol. 69, Italian American Studies, $12

FRED GARDAPHÉ, *Moustache Pete is Dead! Long Live Moustache Pete!*, Vol. 67, Literature/Oral History, $12

PAOLO RUFFILLI, *Dark Room/Camera oscura*, Vol. 66, Poetry, $11

HELEN BAROLINI, *Crossing the Alps*, Vol. 65, Fiction, $14

COSMO FERRARA, *Profiles of Italian Americans*, Vol. 64, Italian American, $16

GIL FAGIANI, *Chianti in Connecticut*, Vol. 63, Poetry, $10

BASSETTI & D'ACQUINO, *Italic Lessons*, Vol. 62, Italian American Studies, $10

CAVALIERI & PASCARELLI, Eds., *The Poet's Cookbook*, Vol. 61, Poetry/Recipes, $12

EMANUEL DI PASQUALE, *Siciliana*, Vol. 60, Poetry, $8

NATALIA COSTA, Ed., *Bufalini*, Vol. 59, Poetry

RICHARD VETERE, *Baroque*, Vol. 58, Fiction

LEWIS TURCO, *La Famiglia/The Family*, Vol. 57, Memoir, $15

NICK JAMES MILETI, *The Unscrupulous*, Vol. 56, Humanities, $20

BASSETTI, ACCOLLA, D'AQUINO, *Italici: An Encounter with Piero Bassetti*, Vol. 55, Italian Studies, $8

GIOSE RIMANELLI, *The Three-legged One*, Vol. 54, Fiction, $15

CHARLES KLOPP, *Bele Antiche Stòrie*, Vol. 53, Criticism, $25

JOSEPH RICAPITO, *Second Wave*, Vol. 52, Poetry, $12

GARY MORMINO, *Italians in Florida*, Vol. 51, History, $15

GIANFRANCO ANGELUCCI, *Federico F.*, Vol. 50, Fiction, $15

ANTHONY VALERIO, *The Little Sailor*, Vol. 49, Memoir, $9

ROSS TALARICO, *The Reptilian Interludes*, Vol. 48, Poetry, $15

RACHEL GUIDO DE VRIES, *Teeny Tiny Tino's Fishing Story*, Vol. 47, Children's Literature, $6

EMANUEL DI PASQUALE, *Writing Anew*, Vol. 46, Poetry, $15

MARIA FAMÀ, *Looking For Cover*, Vol. 45, Poetry, $12

ANTHONY VALERIO, *Toni Cade Bambara's One Sicilian Night*, Vol. 44, Poetry, $10

EMANUEL CARNEVALI, Dennis Barone, Ed., *Furnished Rooms*, Vol. 43, Poetry, $14

BRENT ADKINS, et al., Ed., *Shifting Borders, Negotiating Places*, Vol. 42, Proceedings, $18

GEORGE GUIDA, *Low Italian*, Vol. 41, Poetry, $11

GARDAPHÈ, GIORDANO, TAMBURRI, *Introducing Italian Americana*, Vol. 40, Italian American Studies, $10

DANIELA GIOSEFFI, *Blood Autumn/Autunno di sangue*, Vol. 39, Poetry, $15/$25

FRED MISURELLA, *Lies to Live by*, Vol. 38, Stories, $15

STEVEN BELLUSCIO, *Constructing a Bibliography*, Vol. 37, Italian Americana, $15

ANTHONY J. TAMBURRI, Ed., *Italian Cultural Studies 2002*, Vol. 36, Essays, $18

BEA TUSIANI, *con amore*, Vol. 35, Memoir, $19

FLAVIA BRIZIO-SKOV, Ed., *Reconstructing Societies in the Aftermath of War*, Vol. 34, History, $30

TAMBURRI, et al., Eds., *Italian Cultural Studies 2001*, Vol. 33, Essays, $18

Published by Bordighera, Inc., an independently owned not-for-profit scholarly organization that has no legal affiliation with the University of Central Florida and The John D. Calandra Italian American Institute, Queens College/CUNY.